I Know What Y
A Maggie Kelburn
(Book 1)
By
Gillian Larkin
www.gillianlarkin.co.uk[1]

---

1. http://www.gillianlarkin.co.uk

I Know What You Saw
Prologue

"Please! I'm begging you! Don't do this." The man gasped for air.

The killer silently watched him.

The dying man struggled to breathe. His hands were on his chest, trying to stem the flow of blood. "Help me! Please."

The killer remained quiet.

The dying man fell to the floor. His voice was barely audible now. "You won't get away with this."

The killer waited until the man took his last breath. A flicker of a smile appeared on the killer's face. It was over.

Chapter 1

"I can't help you," the young man said. "Sorry."

Maggie Kelburn didn't think he was sorry at all. "Can't you have a little look, please? I'll pay you."

The young man turned his attention back to his computer screen. "Nope. You didn't buy it from here, so it's not my problem." His blond floppy hair fell over his left eye as he tapped away on his keyboard. Maggie thought she saw a spark of amusement in the one eye she could still see.

She leaned on the counter, kept her voice calm, and said, "The sign in your window says that you do repairs. It doesn't say you only repair items which have been bought from here. Or have I missed that sign?"

The man shrugged in reply, scratched his bearded chin, but didn't look at her.

Maggie's hackles rose. One thing she couldn't bear was bad manners.

She tried again, "Can't you at least take a quick look at it? And tell me if there's a chance it could be repaired. Can't you do that?" She held the small box up. "There's something very important on here. Extremely important."

That got his attention. He swivelled in his chair until he was fully facing her. For the first time since she'd entered Ward's Surveillance Supplies, he gave her his full attention.

He pushed the hair off his face, quickly looked her over, and said, "Yeah? Something important? Like what?"

"It's of a sensitive nature."

He nodded as if he already knew what was on the recording device. "Cheating husband? Caught him in the act did you?"

"Erm, no." Maggie pulled the black box to her chest, suddenly wary of the glee in his eyes.

"Gossiping neighbours? Saying all sorts of things about you? Spreading colourful rumours about you? Ruining your reputation?"

Maggie took an involuntary step back. "Nothing like that. Perhaps I'll go elsewhere."

The man held his hand up. "I know what it is. Something to do with work. Have you been having an affair with someone?" He tutted at his comments.

" Of course you haven't. Why would you record yourself doing that? I know! Someone's been stealing from you. That's it. Someone you've trusted for years has betrayed you. And you caught them in the act on your little recording device. And now your heart is full of pain, and the only thing that will make you feel better is by reporting the black-hearted thief to the police."

Maggie gasped. "No! Nothing like that. You've got a very suspicious mind."

"Thanks. Let me have a look at that box."

Maggie backed up. "No. Thank you. I made a mistake coming here. Sorry to waste your time. Goodbye."

She jumped as someone put a hand on her shoulder. A voice behind her said, "You're not leaving."

Chapter 2

"Get your hand off me!" Maggie spun around and came face-to-face with a man dressed in a smart, dark blue business suit. He was tall and slim. But slim in that athletic kind of way as if he liked exercising.

The man took his hand off her shoulder and smiled at her. "Sorry for startling you. I didn't mean to." The lines around his brown eyes crinkled up. "I caught the back end of your conversation with Jake over there. I can't let you leave my shop without looking at your recording device. That's what it is, isn't it?"

Maggie abruptly shoved the black box into her handbag. "I don't want you to look at it now. Not after what that young man thinks could be on it."

A dark look came into the man's eyes. He looked over at Jake. "Yes, I did hear his suggestions. And I'll be having words with him later."

Maggie heard a snort of derision coming from Jake. It was followed by a tapping noise and a small amount of mumbling from the young man.

The man in front of Maggie smiled again. He said, "I apologise on Jake's behalf. Shall we start again? I'm Sam Ward. I own this business. How can I help you?"

Maggie hesitated. She wanted to leave this place as quickly as possible and return home. But there was something in Sam's eyes which made her think she could trust him. Even that was silly because she'd only just met him. He looked about her age, perhaps a bit younger, so maybe he would understand why she'd used this recording device. Or, at least, he'd have the good manners not to mock her when he found out who she'd been spying on.

Sam must have caught her hesitation because he looked over at Jake and said, "Why don't you go out for your lunch?"

Jake replied shortly, "I've already had my lunch."

"Have another." Sam's reply was more of an order than a suggestion. He looked back at Maggie, and said, "Come with me, please. I'll have a look at your recording device free of charge. If you will allow me to?"

Maggie gave him a tight-lipped smile. "I suppose that would be okay. I recorded something last night, and I'd like to look at it." She handed the black box to Sam. "I'm afraid it's a bit damaged."

4

Sam didn't say anything as he looked at the teeth marks on the box. He walked over to the counter, and looked at Jake until the young man stood up and said, "I'll go for my second lunch then, shall I?"

"You do that," Sam replied with a smile. "Take your time. Oh, switch the coffee machine on before you go. Thanks."

Jake muttered something under his breath before leaving the room through a side door.

"I just can't get the staff," Sam said to Maggie, his eyes twinkling. He walked around to the chair which Jake had just vacated and pulled it out. "Would you like to take a seat while I look at this device? It won't take me long to make an assessment."

Maggie hesitated. She wasn't sure she wanted him to look at it now. He would laugh at her. Or worse, he would be really polite and not laugh.

Sam pulled the chair out a bit further. "I'll make you a coffee. We have excellent coffee here. And I'll open the good biscuits. The ones with chocolate on them." He waggled his eyebrows at her.

Despite her anguish, Maggie laughed. "Okay. Thank you." She took a seat.

"Won't be a moment," Sam told her. He disappeared through the same door which Jake had used and returned two minutes later with coffee and biscuits. True to his word, they were good biscuits and had a satisfying thick layer of chocolate on them.

Once the coffee and biscuits had been handed out, Sam sat down in a chair next to her and asked, "Can I take your name, please? Unless you don't want to, that is. A lot of my customers wish to remain anonymous." He smiled. Maggie noticed he did a lot of that.

"It's Maggie. Maggie Kelburn." She took a quick look around the surveillance shop. There were tall glass cabinets at either side. Some of the cabinets had various devices in them. They looked like the recording devices she'd seen online. Other cabinets had everyday items in them like air fresheners, electrical sockets, calculators, and belts. Were those recording devices too? The shop was brightly lit and seemed almost clinical. Not that welcoming at all. But, for some reason, she'd been drawn to this shop.

Her curiosity rose. What sort of people came in here? What did they buy? She was tempted to ask Sam but didn't want to appear nosy.

Sam was looking at the black box. Using a tiny tool, he carefully prised the box open. He extracted something small and square from inside it. "Great. The main part hasn't been damaged. Let's see the footage." He plugged it into the side of a laptop.

Maggie almost choked on her biscuit. She so didn't want him to see what she'd recorded now. "Wait!"

Too late.

Sam was staring at the screen. His mouth was hanging open.

Chapter 3

Sam closed his mouth, looked at Maggie and said, "Hedgehogs?"

Maggie's cheeks burned with embarrassment. She focused her eyes on the biscuit she'd just picked up. "Yes. Hedgehogs."

Sam repeated, "Hedgehogs?"

Was he mocking her?

Maggie looked his way. She had nothing to be embarrassed about. "Yes! Hedgehogs. So what?"

"Oh, nothing." Sam blinked. "Is there a reason you were recording hedgehogs?"

Maggie pressed her lips together. She could tell by the look in his eyes he thought she was a madwoman. "I was recording them to prove they are real. Of course."

He blinked again. "But they are real. Everyone knows that." He looked as if he were going to say something else, but then thought better of it.

"I had to record them. I told my neighbours I had a family of hedgehogs living in my back garden, but they wouldn't believe me. They said hedgehogs wouldn't make their home in a garden like mine, not at this time of the year, but I said they had. I'd seen them. They thought I was going mad. So I had to prove it to them." She paused for a second. "Not to prove that I was going mad, but about the hedgehogs. And I wanted to see what they were up to. I like hedgehogs."

Sam gave her a slow nod. "I see."

Maggie let out a heavy sigh and made to stand up. "You think I'm a bored housewife with nothing better to do with my time. Sorry to waste your time."

"I don't think that at all." Sam pointed to the screen. "That food and water there, did you put it out for the hedgehogs?"

Maggie nodded.

"That was thoughtful of you," Sam said with a smile. "Sit back down. Let's look at these lovely creatures together. I'm a fan of hedgehogs too."

"I should go."

"Look! There's a baby one there."

"Where?" Maggie sat down and rolled her chair closer to Sam's. She smiled as she saw a little nose sniffing the recording box.

A huge, open mouth suddenly appeared behind the baby hedgehog.

"It's that fox!" Maggie cried out. "I knew it had been bothering those hedgehogs. Get away!" She flapped her hands at the screen even though it was a useless thing to do.

"It's okay. The hedgehog has rolled itself into a ball. What's happening now?"

They watched as the fox clamped its teeth on the box.

"Ah, that's why there are teeth marks on the casing," Sam said. He frowned. "Where's the fox going now?"

"That's my street," Maggie replied indignantly. "The cheeky thing! Not only did that fox terrorise the hedgehogs, he stole my property too."

Sam shook his head. "The scoundrel. We should report him to the police. I can print out an image of his face. Put posters up around town. We'll catch the wily creature."

Maggie looked at Sam. "Are you making fun of me?"

"Not at all." He gave her a considered look. "It makes a nice change for me to see footage like this, instead of—" He stopped talking. "You don't want to know."

Maggie did want to know. She couldn't help it if she was the curious type. It was just in her nature.

They watched the screen as the fox made his way down Maggie's street. He turned into a garden and padded along the path. Then he dropped the box. Maggie and Sam saw the fox walking away.

"That's number forty-eight," Maggie said. "A man moved in there a few weeks ago."

"Is that where you found your device?"

Maggie shook her head. "No. It was on the road just outside my house. I saw the teeth marks on it and assumed an animal had moved it. I thought the device was broken, so that's why I brought it here." She focused on the image on the screen.

The recording device was aimed at the living room window of the house of number forty-eight. They could see a man moving about inside.

"That's my neighbour. I've only spoken to him once." She shifted in her seat. "I don't like spying on him. It feels weird."

Sam's eyes widened as he stared at the screen. He said, "Things are starting to get a lot weirder."

Chapter 4

After watching the footage four more times, Maggie said quietly, "I don't know whether I want to be sick or if I'm going to faint."

Sam gave her a concerned look. "You can use the staff bathroom if you're going to be sick. Perhaps another biscuit might help, you know, for the shock."

Maggie nodded, and reached for another biscuit. Her hand shook as she picked it up. She looked at it. Her stomach lurched, and she dropped the biscuit. "I can't eat. I don't think I'll be eating anything for a long time."

They stared at the frozen image on the screen and didn't say anything for a full minute.

Maggie broke the silence by saying, "Have we really witnessed a murder? Right there, on my street?"

"It looks that way."

Maggie sat up straighter. "There must be something wrong with the camera. That's it. It was one of the cheaper models. Yes. That's what's wrong."

Sam gave her a long look. "The camera doesn't lie. Sorry to use a cliché."

"But it must be faulty! My street doesn't have murders. It's a quiet street. With quiet people who mind their own business. People who always take their bins in as soon as they've been emptied. People who take a package in if you're not at home." Panic rose in her. "We don't have murders in my street! We just don't!"

"Murders happen more frequently than you think," Sam said softly. "In my line of business, I see a lot of crime. Do you want some water? Some fresh air? You've gone pale. Take some deep breaths."

Maggie couldn't let go of her panic. She waved her hand at the screen. "That must be old footage. Someone must have owned this recording device before, recorded that horrible crime, and then sent it back to the company I bought it from."

"Why would they do that?"

Maggie thought for a second. "It's the perfect crime! That's it. A murder is witnessed by someone, maybe an accomplice, but now there's no evidence of it because I've recorded my hedgehogs over it." She gave Sam an overly bright smile. "Well, I've recorded most of my hedgehogs over it."

Sam surprised her by placing his hand over hers. It was pleasantly warm. He said, "Maggie, you know that doesn't make sense. You told me this is your street, and this recording was done last night. The date confirms it." He glanced towards the screen, and then back at her. "Is that your neighbour?"

Maggie blinked rapidly as if that would make the awful truth go away.

"Maggie, please look at him."

She did so. Her heart sank as the dreadful realisation of what they'd seen washed over her. Her eyes suddenly stung. She gave Sam a brief nod.

"Okay. It's okay." Sam still had his hand over hers. "Now that we have this recording, we have to do something with it."

Maggie jumped to her feet. "Of course! We have to show it to the police right now. That poor man could still be alive and fighting for his last breath."

"I doubt it," Sam said with a grimace. "We saw him dying."

"We don't know that for certain. He just fell from view. He could be lying on his carpet right now, needing help. Give me that device. I'll get it over to the police station right now." She held her hand out.

"Just a minute." Sam tapped away on his computer for a few seconds. Then he took the device out of the side of his computer and placed it inside a small metal box. He put the chewed-up casing in too. "Maggie, you have to—"

She took the metal container. "I have to get to the police station immediately! Yes, I know. Thanks for your help." Her smile was too bright. "The police will sort this out. Then my lovely, quiet street will be back to normal again. Goodbye! Thanks for your help."

She made to turn away, but Sam stood up and put his hand on her shoulder. "Maggie, I was about to say you need to be careful. You now have evidence that a murder occurred in your street."

"Yes, I know that. But the police will sort it out. And the sooner I get to the station, the better. Thanks again for your help."

Sam's voice was firm as he said, "Maggie, where there's a murder, there will be at least one murderer. And that murderer could have been watching your street to make sure no one saw their crime."

Maggie swallowed. She didn't like where this conversation was going.

Sam continued. "That murderer could have seen you picking the recording device up early today. They could have followed you here."

Maggie's knees buckled, and she fell heavily to the chair beneath her. She would have missed it completely if Sam hadn't put his arms around her just in time and guided her into it.

He sat back in his chair, looked straight into her eyes, and said, "Whoever murdered your neighbour could know about your recording device. And if so, they'll try to stop you going to the police."

Maggie's vision swam slightly. Her voice was barely above a whisper as she said, "No. That doesn't happen to people like me. I'm just a normal woman, who likes hedgehogs." She turned fear-filled eyes Sam's way. "Am I in danger?"

Chapter 5

Maggie fought hard to keep herself together. Sam made her another coffee and insisted she eat at least one biscuit. Maggie tried, but it tasted like dust in her mouth.

She said to Sam, "My head is full of images of all the TV shows I've watched. I keep thinking that murders can't take place in quiet places, but they can, and they do. Don't they?"

Sam nodded in reply. "Let the police deal with this. They know what to do. But just to put my mind at rest, let me come with you to the police station."

Maggie's eyes widened. She cast a glance at the exit door, and whispered, "Do you think the murderer is waiting for me outside?"

"I could lie and say no, but there's a small possibility that someone could have followed you. They probably haven't, but you never know." He let out a small laugh. "Actually, I do know from experience that these things happen."

Maggie shook her head at him. "What kind of a world do you live in?"

The main door suddenly opened. Maggie screamed, threw herself out of the chair and hid under the desk.

"What's wrong with her?" said a voice she recognised. It was Jake.

With as much dignity as she could muster, Maggie stood up, smoothed down her jacket and gave Jake a small smile. "I thought I'd dropped something under the table."

Sam said, "Maggie, it's okay. You don't have to lie to Jake."

Jake looked from Maggie to Sam. A hard expression came into his young face. He addressed Sam directly. "What's happened?"

Sam stood up, and said, "A murder."

Jake sighed. "Another one? So soon?

"What do you mean, another one?" Maggie asked.

Jake ignored her and moved over to Sam. "Do we know who was murdered?"

"No," Sam replied. "It's one of Maggie's neighbours. She caught it on her recording device."

"By accident," Maggie defended herself. "I didn't set out to record a vicious crime."

Jake took his phone out and looked at it. "When did we last do a sweep?"

Sam checked his phone too. "I did one this morning when I first came in. You?"

"Thirty-three minutes ago. I'll do another. I'll check the CCTV cameras too." He walked into the room at the side, still looking at his phone.

Maggie said, "What's going on? What's all this business about a sweep? Are you getting the vacuum out? I appreciate your attitude to cleanliness, but I think we should go to the police station now. If you still want to come with me?"

"I do." Sam put his phone away. "Because of the people we deal with here, and their issues, we perform security sweeps often. And we've got CCTV aimed at many places around the building: inside and out."

Maggie was at a loss for words. For a second. "It's like I've walked into a parallel universe."

"Welcome to my world," Sam said with a small smile. "A world full of crime, suspicion and treachery."

"But it pays the bills!" Jake announced as he came back into the room. "I've done a sweep. It's all clear. Outside is clear too. Just the usual suspects walking about."

"The usual suspects?" Maggie asked fearfully. "Who's out there?"

Jake's expression softened. "Sorry. That was the wrong thing to say. I meant just the normal people who are out at this time of the day. People shopping or going to work."

"Right. I see." Maggie let out a sharp laugh. "So, no murderers lurking in dark corners waiting for me? Ready to silence me, just as they silenced my neighbour? No mastermind criminals, possibly in disguise, ready to whack me on the head and steal my handbag?"

Jake looked like he was considering the matter. He opened his mouth to say something, but Sam brusquely stopped him by saying, "Right. Let's get to the police station. Jake, we shouldn't be too long. Keep doing the sweeps and the other things. Okay?"

Jake sighed. "Okay. I know what to do. This isn't the first murder we've dealt with."

Maggie wasn't sure if that made her feel better or not.

A minute later, she was standing on the street outside Ward's Surveillance Supplies.

The world looked different somehow.

People looked different.

She felt different.

She'd witnessed a murder. And now her life could be in danger.

"Erm, Sam?" She cleared her throat. "Is it okay if I call you Sam?"

"Of course. What's wrong?" He indicated for her to start walking.

She did so but kept looking nervously left and right. "Will the police deal with everything?"

"Yes."

"Will my street be a safe place again?"

"Is anywhere ever completely safe?"

She winced. "I suppose not."

They walked on.

"Erm, Sam."

"Yes?"

"Will the police catch the murderer? Are they good at doing that? It's not something I've considered before. Well, you don't, do you?"

Sam didn't reply.

"Sam? Did you hear me?"

They stopped at a crossing, and waited for the green man to appear. Sam looked straight into her eyes, and said, "I did hear you. I have to be honest. The police don't always catch the murderer."

A series of beeps let them know the green man had appeared. They crossed the road.

When they reached the other side, Maggie said quietly, "Do you think they'll catch the person who killed my neighbour?"

With a grim smile, Sam answered, "I hope so."

They reached the police station. Just before they went inside, Maggie felt the back of her neck prickle.

It almost felt like someone was watching her.

Chapter 6

Maggie had never been into a police station before. She didn't know what to expect or where to go. Luckily, Sam took charge and led her over to a large desk just inside the entrance.

The middle-aged police officer behind the desk gave them a tiny smile in welcome. She was tall, with blonde hair pulled back from her face.

Maggie looked left and right at the few people who were sitting on a row of chairs. She whispered to Sam, "Will we go somewhere private? I don't want to talk about, you know what, in front of everyone."

Sam only nodded in reply, and gently pushed her in front of him so she could talk to the woman behind the desk.

Maggie noticed the woman's attention went to Sam for a second, and she gave him an almost imperceptible nod. Did they know each other?

The woman spoke, "Good morning. What can I help you with?"

Having never reported a murder before, Maggie didn't know the best way to begin. So, she blurted out, "I've recorded a murder! By accident. The recording was an accident. Not the murder. Not by the look of it. I think he was murdered on purpose." She paused when she heard the shuffling of bottoms on chairs as if the people behind her were getting into a better listening position.

The police officer didn't seem at all surprised by Maggie's words. She merely nodded, picked up a pen, and said, "Could you give me more details, please? Address. Names. Times. How the crime was committed?"

Maggie felt sweat breaking out on her forehead. Seeing her neighbour being stabbed repeatedly in the chest with a sharp implement, and then falling out of view was one thing: trying to describe it in detail to a stranger was something else altogether. She wasn't sure she wanted to voice the words.

Sam came to her rescue. He said, "The incident was recorded. We have the footage. We didn't get any audio as the device doesn't have that facility." He paused and looked at Maggie for a moment. "The victim's injury is clearly seen, as is his face when he is struck. Unfortunately, the person who killed him never came into view, apart from a gloved hand."

"Where's the recording device now?" the police officer asked.

With a hand which shook a little, Maggie took the metal box from her bag and gave it to the officer.

"We'll have a good look at this," the officer said. "If it's something we need to investigate, then we'll take this further."

Maggie let out a gasp of surprise. "What do you mean 'if'? There's been a murder on my street! My neighbour is probably lying in a pool of blood as we speak. You have to send someone around there right now!"

A cold look came into the police officer's eyes. "We have procedures. This isn't the first time we've been given footage of a supposed murder. We've had many hoaxes from members of the public who have nothing better to do with their time." She opened the box and looked inside. "And they usually use cheap recording devices like this one."

Maggie's mouth dropped open in shock.

Sam interjected. "The footage seems genuine to me. As does Ms Kelburn here. You are going to take her details, aren't you? You can do that, at least."

The officer snapped the box closed and gave Sam a withering look. "Trying to tell us how to do our jobs again, Mr Ward?"

Sam folded his arms in response and said nothing.

Maggie's eyes narrowed at the exchange. What was going on here?

The police officer looked at Maggie and snapped, "Full name. Address. Date of birth. And don't lie about your age."

"I wasn't going to," Maggie said in a small voice. Was there any need for such animosity?

Maggie proceeded to give her details. The police officer was either a bit deaf or purposely being irksome because she kept asking Maggie to speak up. This resulted in Maggie almost shouting her private details out, and to a room where total strangers were listening to her every word.

By the time they'd been coldly dismissed by the police officer, Maggie was shaking as if she'd been mentally abused. She almost ran out of the station. Sam quickly followed her.

Once outside, Maggie leaned against the wall and said, "That was awful. Do the police treat everyone like that?"

"Only the ones I've been married to," Sam said. "That was my ex-wife. And possibly the worst person you could have spoken to. I'm so sorry. I should have checked first to make sure Ingrid wasn't working. Are you okay?"

His ex-wife? Maggie pushed herself away from the wall. "I think so. What's going to happen now? Will they take the footage seriously?"

"Oh, yes, of course," Sam said in a confidant manner. But his eyes said something else.

Maggie cast an uncertain look at the police station as they walked away. She suddenly didn't have any confidence in the police.

Chapter 7

Maggie and Sam were silent as they headed back to the surveillance shop. Maggie wanted to ask Sam a million questions, mainly ones about his ex-wife, and why she was his ex-wife. But it wasn't the sort of thing you asked someone you'd only recently met.

They stopped at the door to Ward's Surveillance Supplies and gave each other uncertain smiles.

Maggie said, "I'd better be going home then. I've got lots to do."

Worry flickered in Sam's eyes. "Shall I come with you?"

"Why?"

"To make sure you're safe."

"Why wouldn't I be safe?" Maggie already knew the answer to that but didn't want to admit it. "The police are dealing with everything now. Or making a start on it anyway."

"Yeah. Right." Sam looked in the direction they'd just come from. He looked back at Maggie, and asked, "How well did you know your neighbour?"

"Not well at all. I think he moved in a few weeks ago. Number forty-eight has been empty for ages, and then one day, there was a man coming out of the front door. I was walking along the street when he came out. He was looking at his bins in confusion."

"His bins?"

"Yes. We've got green ones, brown ones and even blue ones. You know, for all the different recycling options. Don't you have them?"

Sam frowned. "We've only got a green one and a black one. What's the blue one for?"

"Glass." She flapped a hand at him. "But that doesn't matter. The man was looking at his bins, and I shouted out a hello, and said the green bin needs to be put out the following day."

Sam's mouth twitched at the corner. "Are you one of those neighbours who knows which bin goes out every week?"

Maggie bristled slightly. "Yes. So? Anyway, the man said thank you, patted his green bin, and went back inside. That's the only time I spoke to him. His house is mainly surrounded by trees, except for the kitchen window which I can see from my living room. I saw him moving about in his kitchen a few times. I never saw him leave the house again, though."

"And did he put the green bin out?"

Maggie's eyes narrowed. "Are you mocking me? Do you think I spend all my time spying on my neighbours?"

"Of course not."

Maggie couldn't tell if he was joking or not.

Sam continued, "Did you get a good look at him? I don't suppose you did if you only spoke a few words to him."

"He was a bit taller than you. On the plump side, but not fat, more of a cuddly physique. He had dark ginger hair cut in a short style, with flecks of grey at the sides. His eyes were dark brown, not mid-brown likes yours. I'd put his age at late fifties, maybe early sixties. His face looked careworn and weathered, and he had a lot of wrinkles around his eyes. When he spoke, he had a thick Scottish accent. Also, he had a dark mole on his left cheek about an inch from the tip of his nose."

Sam stared at Maggie.

She gave him a satisfied nod. Then she frowned. "I should have told the police that. But your ex-wife didn't ask. You can see most of his features on the footage, but she won't know how tall he is, or about his accent. Should I go back to the police station?"

Sam found his voice. "No. Yes. I mean, just leave it for now. You're very observant. Are you like this with everyone? Remembering details about them?"

"I'm interested in people. I always have been. And I just seem to remember things. Not always names, but what people look like." She gave him a wry smile. "I used to think that if there was a crime on my street, and the police came to my door to ask if I'd seen anything suspicious, I'd be able to say yes, and then give them a full account of the dubious characters I'd seen hanging around."

"You still can. Why don't you give the police a few hours to make their initial investigations, and then chase them up? You can give them a full description of your neighbour too. I know from experience that if you keep pestering them, they will do something."

"Won't they get annoyed with me?"

Sam nodded. "Definitely. But we saw a murder, and something has to be done." He cleared his throat. "Can I take your phone number? Then you can let me know how you get on. I know it's nothing to do with me, but..." He trailed off and gave her a shrug. "I'd like to know."

Maggie nodded. "Of course. I'd like you to know too. I'll take your number too." She glanced at the name above the shop. "Oh, it's up there. Shall I use that one?"

"No, that's business only. I'll give you my private one."

They swapped numbers. For some reason, having Sam's number made Maggie feel somewhat safer.

"I'd better be off then," Maggie said.

"Is there anyone at home?" Sam asked. "Anyone for you to talk to? Like a husband?"

"No husband. Not anymore. But my son, Oscar, phones or texts me almost every day." She pressed her lips together for a moment. "I'm not sure I want to tell him about the murder. He'd only worry, and tell me to leave the house. He'd probably want me to go live with him in Newcastle until the police caught the murderer."

"Would that be a bad idea? You'd be safe there."

Maggie considered the matter. "I'll be safe in my own house. I always have been." She noticed the worry in his eyes. "I can take care of myself. I have done for years. Thanks again for your help."

Sam put his hand on her elbow. "Don't do anything stupid, will you?"

"Like what?"

He took his hand back. "Like investigating this on your own. Don't do that."

Maggie made a weird noise which was a mixture of a snort and a laugh. "Of course I won't do that. What kind of a person do you think I am?"

Chapter 8

Maggie did try her best to walk past number forty-eight. She really did. But she failed.

Maybe just one little peep through the window, she told herself. That won't hurt, will it? Just to see if her neighbour was lying there. And if he was, then she'd phone the police immediately and tell them. It was her duty as a concerned citizen to check on him.

Once she'd convinced herself she was doing the right thing, Maggie opened the garden gate of number forty-eight and walked along the path. The murder had taken place in the living room, so she went that way.

It was only when she was inches away from the window that she realised she didn't want to see a dead body. What was she thinking? Why would anyone want to see the murdered body of a neighbour?

She turned around, paused, and then turned back. But what if he were still alive? He'd need urgent help.

Maggie moved closer to the window, and carefully inched her face forward until she could see inside. She steeled herself for whatever came into view.

A woman's face suddenly appeared in front of her.

"Arghh!" Maggie screamed and clutched her chest.

The woman inside rapped loudly on the window, and yelled, "Who are you? What do you want?"

Before Maggie could think of an excuse, the woman vanished from view and appeared a minute later at the open front door. "Oi! You! Nosy Parker! What do you want? I'm not buying anything. And I'm not joining any religious cults."

Maggie patted her chest in an effort to slow her racing heart. She managed to put a smile on her face as she walked towards the woman. "I'm so sorry. I didn't mean to scare you."

"You didn't scare me. I don't scare that easily." The woman folded her arms and gave Maggie a suspicious look. "Well? What do you want?"

Maggie regarded the woman for a moment. She was elderly, but not at all frail. Her hair was grey and set in tight curls. Her eyes were sizing Maggie up.

An idea suddenly came to Maggie. It wasn't an amazing idea, but it would have to do. "I live a few houses down. I got a card through my letterbox saying I'd missed a delivery and the package had been left with a neighbour. But the card didn't say which neighbour." Maggie tutted and rolled her eyes dramatically. "You know what those delivery people are like."

"I haven't got your parcel." The woman's suspicious look grew more intense. "And why didn't you knock on the door like a normal person instead of looking through the window?"

Maggie tried to look indignant. "I did knock. You mustn't have heard me."

"You didn't knock. I've got hearing as sharp as a bat's."

Maggie ignored her harsh tone. She looked over the woman's shoulder, and into the hallway behind. "Are you sure you haven't got my package? Perhaps it was delivered when you were out. Maybe that man took it in."

The woman moved to the middle of the doorway so that she was blocking Maggie's view. "I haven't been out. And what man? There aren't any men in my house. And don't you go spreading rumours that there is. You look the type to spread rumours."

"But there was a man here. I spoke to him about the bins. He's about this tall." Maggie held her hand up. "Ginger hair. Scottish. A mole on his cheek. I saw him a few weeks ago."

"A mole? Ginger hair? Scottish? No, there's no one like that here. Never has been, and never will be." She gave Maggie a dismissive sniff. "Are you sure you didn't dream this up just so you could have a nosy through my window? You look the nosy type."

Anger flashed through Maggie. "I'm not making it up. I saw him. I told him to put his green bin out!"

"Maybe you were talking to one of the other neighbours. What time of the day did this happen? At night? Were you drunk? You look the type who gets drunk often."

"I do not get drunk often!" Maggie exploded. "I saw him. I spoke to him. And I saw him moving around the kitchen when I looked out of my window! I can see your kitchen from my house."

"You've been spying on me when I'm in the kitchen? That's outrageous! I'm going to phone the police. Get off my property!"

"The police will be coming here anyway. To check on the footage I recorded. Of the hedgehogs, the fox, and the—" Maggie stopped talking. She didn't want to mention the murder.

The elderly woman said firmly, "I'm closing the door now. I think you should seek medical advice. Urgently." She closed the door. Maggie heard the door being locked.

Maggie didn't move for a few seconds. What was going on here? Where had the Scottish man gone? He was definitely here a few weeks ago. And, according to the video footage, he was here last night.

This didn't make any sense.

Maggie slowly walked away.

And who was that woman? Maggie had never seen her before.

She was still trying to make sense of it all as she made her way along the street and towards her house. As she went inside, her phone rang. She quickly answered it thinking it was the police.

But it wasn't.

Chapter 9

"Mum! Hi!"

Maggie smiled as she walked towards her kitchen. "Oscar. Hi. How are you? How's work going? Did you make a start on that new project you told me about? That one about recycling more plastic?" She held the phone between her chin and neck while taking her coat off.

"Never mind me. What about you? How's Brighton? Are you having a great time?"

Maggie looked out of her kitchen window. "Erm, well—"

"Have you been on that viewing tower thing yet? That really high one? Did you take any photos?" He laughed. "I bet you've been on a tour bus. You love those buses. You always made us go on them when we went on holiday."

"Well, I—" Maggie moved towards the kettle, checked the water level, and switched it on.

"You must have been to the Royal Pavilion by now. And what about The Lanes with its eclectic mix of shops?"

Maggie frowned. "Are you looking at something online about Brighton?"

"Yep. Hang on, let me scroll down this blog post. Have you been on the famous Brighton Palace Pier? Oh, just a minute. There's some pictures of that other pier too, that one that's crumbling into the sea. It looks like a ghost pier. Take some photos of that when you see it."

Maggie opened the fridge, looked at a wine bottle wistfully, and then reached for the milk. It was far too early to be drinking, despite the shocking day she'd had.

"Oscar, I've got something to tell you."

He took a sharp intake of breath. "Don't tell me you went to the nudist beach, Mum. There's a warning online about that. Did you stumble on it by accident? I hope you closed your eyes."

"Oscar, listen to me."

"Oh no! You didn't take your clothes off and join the others, did you? Mum, tell me you didn't do that. Please."

"I didn't do that. I didn't do any of it. Because I'm not in Brighton. I'm still in Leeds." She took a tea bag out of the caddy and put it in her favourite cup.

She could feel Oscar's disapproval over the line and knew he was trying to find a kind way to berate her. It took him a while, and Maggie managed to make herself a cup of tea, open a packet of crisps, and take herself into the living room before he spoke again.

"Mum, why didn't you go? After what Carmella said to you? It was so kind of her to offer you that holiday. And for free too. I can't believe it. I just can't."

"You're being judgmental," Maggie said. "You told me to point that out if you ever did it again. What was it you said? Something about kind words leading to kind deeds. Are you being kind to your old mum right now?"

Oscar sighed over the phone. "I'm trying. But I've been picturing you having a great time in Brighton. I'm not trying to nag, but you have to get out, Mum. You can't stay inside forever. You're becoming a hermit. I know you miss Dad. I do too. But you've still got a life to live."

Maggie's eyes prickled. "Let's not talk about your dad, please. I didn't want to go to Brighton, and that's that."

"But why not?"

Maggie knew why not, but she wasn't going to admit that to Oscar. She wasn't going to tell him she wasn't brave enough to go away on her own. "I've got too much to do here. I'm still looking for another job, for a start."

"But Dad left you plenty of money. You don't have to work."

"But I like working." Maggie put the crisp packet on the table. Her appetite had vanished for the second time that day. "I like being around people."

"I worry about you. All alone in that house all day. I keep thinking you'll end up talking to the walls. I saw a movie about a woman who did that."

"I haven't started talking to the walls," Maggie admitted. She didn't tell him she'd been talking to her hedgehog visitors every night. He didn't need to know that.

"But what about Carmella? What will she think? Does she know you haven't gone to Brighton? She'll be upset to know you've thrown her gift back in her face. I should come back to Leeds, and talk to her. Apologise on your behalf."

Anger rushed through Maggie. She was feeling a lot of unaccustomed anger today. "No one is going to apologise for me. I make my own decisions. Don't tell me how to behave. I'm the parent. Remember?"

Oscar was quick to apologise. "I'm sorry. You're right. We're all free to live the life we want. Is Carmella at home anyway? I haven't seen her for a while. If I come home to see you, I could call in and say hello to her. She's always so interested in my work."

Maggie smiled. Her son had a very obvious crush on her vibrant neighbour. She couldn't resist saying, "She's never going to marry you, you know. She's decades older than you."

"Some women like younger men," Oscar defended himself. "Is she at home?"

"No. She's gone off on one of those soul and spirit festivals again."

"Oh? When will she be back?"

"In a week or two." Maggie's smile widened. "So, are you still coming home to see me?"

"Maybe in a week or two. I have to go, Mum. I've got a meeting. Is there anything you want to talk about? I can phone back after my meeting."

Maggie paused for a fraction of a second. "No."

Oscar laughed. "Nothing exciting happening on the street?"

"No."

"Okay. I'll speak to you later. You know I only worry because I love you so much."

"I know. But I'm the parent, and it's my job to worry about you. It's not the other way around. Love you too. Speak soon."

They said goodbye and ended the call.

Maggie cradled the cup of tea in her hands and leaned back in the armchair. Should she have told him about the murder? Should she phone him later on when he'd finished work and tell him then?

A sudden noise cut through her thoughts.

She sat up straighter.

What was that?

The noise came to her again. It was a squeaking, creaking noise. A familiar noise.

It was the gate at the bottom of the back garden. No one ever used the gate because it squeaked so much. She must remember to oil it someday.

With trembling hands, Maggie put her cup down and headed for the kitchen. She walked fearfully towards the window.

A sudden movement caught her eye near the bottom of the garden.

She held back her scream as she stared at the hooded figure who was crouched near the gate.

The hooded figure lifted his head and looked straight at her.

Chapter 10

Maggie quickly ducked, her heart beating like thunder in her ears.

Who was that?

What was he doing in her garden?

Was it the killer?

Had he found out about the footage?

What was he going to do now?

Maggie broke out in a sweat. These things didn't happen to someone like her. They just didn't.

But it was happening. She had witnessed a murder, and now there was a stranger in her garden. What was she supposed to do?

She quickly glanced around the kitchen. What could she use as a weapon to defend herself? A knife? She shuddered. She didn't think she'd be able to stab someone. And anyway, the knives were in a wooden block near the kitchen window. She'd have to stand up to get one, and the killer would see her.

What else could she use? There was a whisk on the table. Would that be any good? What damage could a whisk cause? Oh! The rolling pin. It was in a drawer just to her left. She could use that. And there were some mixing bowls in there too. They could be useful for—

KNOCK! KNOCK!

The killer was at the kitchen door!

Maggie clutched her chest, convinced she was going to have a heart attack at any second.

The police! She had to phone the police. But her phone was in the other room.

On her knees, Maggie shuffled into the living room and headed for her phone.

Someone was looking right at her through the window.

Maggie froze in fear.

The man tapped lightly on the glass and smiled at her.

It was Sam. He smiled again and gave her a friendly wave. He was wearing a hooded top. It had been him lurking in the back garden.

Relief rushed through Maggie. Quickly followed by anger.

She got to her feet, marched over to the front door and yanked it open. "What the heck are you doing? You idiot. You scared me half to death. Why were you prowling around my garden like an evil murderer?"

"I—"

"And was that you knocking at my kitchen door? Why would you do that? Do you know how loud you were? Have you got fists made of steel?"

"I—"

Maggie planted her hands on her hips. "I was ready to whack you on the head with a rolling pin. And I was going to whisk you!"

"Whisk me?" Sam's mouth twitched slightly.

"Don't you dare laugh at me. Not after what you've just done to me."

"I wouldn't dare laugh at you." He put one hand on his chest. "I am truly sorry for scaring you. I didn't mean to."

"Why did you go in my back garden then? What were you up to?"

"I wanted to talk to you."

"About what? And why didn't you use the front door?"

Sam averted his gaze. "I thought I'd have a quick look at the hedgehogs. They are in the back garden, aren't they?" He looked back at her.

"They are. But you could have come to the front door and asked to see them."

Sam looked over his shoulder, and to the street behind him. "You're right. But I wanted to check your property too." He paused, and then looked back at her. "To see where your escape routes are. To see where you could go if you had to leave your house quickly."

Maggie frowned. "Why would I have to do that?"

Sam averted his gaze again. "It's always useful to know these things. Just in case."

Maggie could sense there was a lot he wanted to tell her, but he was reluctant to do so. Why would she ever need to leave her house quickly? Why would he even think that?

She said, "Why did you want to talk to me? Is it about...you know?" She briefly looked in the direction of number forty-eight.

Sam nodded. "I didn't want to phone you because your phone might not be secure."

Maggie stared at him. "What?"

"Your phone. It might not be secure."

Maggie involuntarily took a step back. There was something wrong with this man. And now she'd got him involved in her life.

She said, "First my house, and now my phone. You're paranoid."

His smile was grim. "I'm only paranoid because they're out to get us."

Maggie put her hand on the door and started to close it. "I've got a lot to do. Goodbye."

Sam took a step forward, lowered his voice, and said, "I've been in touch with the police. Something's happened."

Chapter 11

Maggie grabbed her handbag and coat, and then followed Sam to a plain white van which was parked down the next street.

"Why have you parked here?" she asked him.

He didn't answer.

Maggie asked, "Is it something to do with those escape plans you're so keen on?"

"Something like that." Sam kept looking left and right as they walked as if checking out every house.

He's a very strange man, Maggie thought, a very, very strange man. And I'm getting into a van with him.

Sam opened the passenger door for her.

She bristled. "I can open the door myself. I've been doing it for years."

"I was being polite. Good manners cost nothing." He indicated his head towards the passenger seat. "Are you getting in, or would you like me to close the door so that you can open it yourself?"

Maggie hesitated. "I'm not sure I should get into a van with you. I don't know you well. And, to be honest, you're a bit weird with your escape plans and stuff."

Sam broke into a smile. "At last! You're using your common sense. I was wondering how long it would take you. Of course you shouldn't be getting into a van with me. I could be anyone. You are far too trusting. I saw that from the moment we met. And you shouldn't be so trusting. It will only get you into trouble."

Maggie's hand tightened around her handbag strap. "Am I in trouble now? With you? Are you going to kidnap me?"

Sam considered the matter for a few seconds. "Is it worth it? Would anyone pay a decent amount to get you back?"

"I don't think so. There's Oscar, my son, but he doesn't have a lot of money. My parents don't have much either. And I wouldn't like you to bother them if you do kidnap me. It'll only upset them. And there's my neighbour—" She stopped when she saw the mirth in his eyes. "Are you messing about?"

"A little. But I'm not going to kidnap you. If it makes you feel any better, you can drive. I will even go in the back of the van. It can only be opened from outside. You can lock me in. Would that be better for you?"

Maggie looked across at the driver's seat. "It would."

"Fair enough." He gave her the keys. "I'll get in the back. Let me know when we get to the police station. There's a small car park at the rear of the station." He made a move towards the back of the van.

"Wait," Maggie said. "I think it'll be okay if you drive."

"Are you sure?"

She held the keys out and looked into his eyes. There was something trustworthy about him. Or was he just giving her that impression? She said, "Don't lock my door, and leave the window down in case I need to shout for help. Okay?"

He grinned. "Okay."

A few minutes later, they were heading into Leeds.

Maggie asked, "Why did the police contact you and not me?"

"They didn't contact me. I got in touch with them soon after you left."

"Oh? Why?"

He gave her a quick look before looking back at the road. "I was concerned for your safety. I wanted the police to take the matter seriously, and to deal with it urgently."

"Right. Thanks."

Maggie didn't know what to say. It had been a long time since anyone had been concerned about her. Apart from Oscar who worried about her far too much.

"What did the police say?" Maggie asked. "Have they checked the footage yet? Do they believe it's real?"

Sam came to a stop at a red light. He looked at her, and said, "They don't have the footage anymore."

Chapter 12

"What?" Maggie asked. "What do you mean? What have they done with it?"

The light changed to green, and Sam set off. "They couldn't explain over the phone."

"Did you speak to the same police officer who we saw earlier? Your ex-wife?"

Sam shook his head. "I didn't. I did ask to speak to her, but she'd left for the day. I tried her phone, but Ingrid's not answering. Probably because it's me."

"But what's happened to the footage? I don't understand."

"I don't either. But we soon will."

He pulled into the car park behind the police station.

They were both quiet as they walked inside. Maggie was thankful to see the reception area was now empty.

The police officer behind the desk was an older man with a friendly face. He gave Sam a wide smile. "Hello, stranger. We haven't seen you for a long time. How are you?"

"Hi, Jeff. I'm doing fine. How are you?"

"I can't complain. Well, I could, but who would listen to me?" He burst into jovial laughter. "I take it this isn't a social visit?" He looked towards Maggie and gave her a small nod of greeting.

Sam said, "We called in earlier with a recording device which belongs to Maggie here. We left it with Ingrid."

Jeff let out a low whistle. "I bet that was awkward."

"A little. Anyway, the footage showed a possible murder on Maggie's street."

Jeff let out another whistle. "Wow. Although why that surprises me, I don't know. I've seen more than I want to in this job. I assume Ingrid took all the details?"

"She did." Sam put his hands on the desk. "Jeff, the recording device has gone missing. I phoned twenty minutes ago to see if Ingrid had logged Maggie's details into your system. I spoke to Carol. She said there was no record of it, either on the system or anywhere else. She had a look around, but couldn't find anything."

Jeff scratched his chin. "That is strange. Carol's just nipped out for a bit. Did you talk to Ingrid about it?"

"I phoned, but she didn't answer."

"That's understandable," Jeff said in a wise tone which made Maggie wonder what had gone on with Sam and his ex-wife.

Sam asked, "Can you have another look for it, Jeff? Not that I'm doubting Carol, but it's important."

"Of course I can. What sort of a recording device was it?" His question was directed at Maggie.

"Erm. It was black, and square, and little." Maggie shrugged, not sure what else to say.

Sam abruptly rattled off the make and model of the box including the precise size. He added how the device was now in a metal box which he'd supplied, and again he gave the exact measurements.

Jeff nodded and then proceeded to look around the desk. He opened many drawers but didn't find anything. He said, "I'll give Ingrid a call. She must have put it somewhere." He took a phone from his pocket and tapped the screen.

"Don't let her know I'm here," Sam said. "She won't help if she knows it's me who's chasing this up."

Jeff gave him a look. "I know that. I wasn't born yesterday despite my youthful looks. Hang on. It's ringing." He began to talk to Ingrid.

Sam took Maggie by the elbow and led her away. In a low voice, he said, "Have you told anyone about the footage, and what we saw?"

"No. I did talk to my son, but I didn't tell him." Maggie thought about her visit to number forty-eight, and the elderly woman she'd spoken to. "I did do something," she began.

She was interrupted by Jeff walking over to them. He said, "Ingrid remembers your visit, of course. She hasn't seen the footage, but she logged it onto our system immediately, and put the device in a safe place."

"A safe place?" Sam asked.

Jeff rubbed the back of his neck. "Yes. In a drawer behind the desk. But I've already looked there. The box isn't there."

"But it's been logged onto your system?" Sam said. "Carol checked the system when I phoned her, but she didn't see anything."

"I'll have a look at our files. And I'll ask around to see if anyone else has seen the device." Jeff hurried away through a door. He came back a minute later, and went on the computer. He tapped away, his brow becoming more wrinkled by the second.

Maggie's heart sank. She knew what he was going to say.

And he did. "Sam, I'm sorry, but there's no record of it here. Ingrid is adamant that she logged it in. There's no reason for her to lie to me."

Sam gave him a slow nod as if mulling something over. "Did she tell you how much detail she put on your system?"

"She did. Ms Kelburn's full name and address, and footage of a possible murder at number forty-eight Lilac Lane." He looked at Maggie. "Number forty-eight? Is that right?"

A trickle of fear went down Maggie's spine. She nodded at Jeff, and said, "What does this mean?"

Jeff tried to give her a reassuring smile. "It's probably just our system playing up. Don't you worry about it. The device will show up somewhere."

Sam's voice was tight as he said, "Jeff, be honest with Maggie. She deserves that considering the danger she's now in."

"What danger?" Maggie asked Sam. He didn't answer. She looked at Jeff. "What danger?"

Jeff let out a resigned sigh. "Despite our amazing security systems, it is possible some outside source hacked into our screens and saw your details. They could have deleted them."

"But why would anyone do that? And who would do that?" Maggie swallowed. She suddenly didn't want to hear the answers.

Sam said quietly, "The person who murdered your neighbour could have done this."

"No." Maggie shook her head. "No. Nope. It's not possible. This is a police station. Their system can't get hacked. That's ridiculous! And where's the recording device? Are you going to tell me it's been stolen?"

At that moment, a police officer opened the door behind Jeff and said, "There's no sign of it anywhere."

Maggie's vision blurred. She put her hand on the desk to steady herself. She was finding it hard to breathe. "What does this mean? I don't understand what's going on."

In a reassuring tone, Jeff said, "It could mean the person behind the alleged murder knows someone reported the crime. They know it was you. And where you live. But we've got this under control. There's nothing to worry about."

Maggie saw a muscle in Sam's jaw tighten. He looked as if he were trying to keep ahold on his temper. His voice was cold as he said, "Jeff, there's everything to worry about." He took Maggie by the arm and said, "We have to get out of here right now. You're not safe here."

Maggie tried to resist. "But this is a police station. This is a safe place."

"Not for you. Come on. Quickly."

Maggie let herself be taken out of the station. It was only when they got outside that her knees gave way, and she collapsed.

Chapter 13

Maggie felt herself being carried.

She opened her eyes and looked at Sam. His face was red with exertion. He was the one who was carrying her.

Maggie's cheeks grew hot. "Sam! Put me down. What are you doing?"

Sam placed her feet first on the ground next to his van. He rubbed his back. "You fainted. Don't you remember?"

Maggie nodded. "Sorry for fainting. It was the shock. You didn't have to carry me. I'm not the lightest of people. Is your back okay?"

"Of course." He continued to rub it. "You're as light as a feather."

"A feather who eats too much chocolate and pizza." She looked towards the police station. "Who would steal that recording device?"

"Apart from the killer? I don't know." He opened the passenger door. "Get in, please. I don't want to talk about this out in the open."

Maggie got in, grabbed a bottle of water from her bag, and took a big swig. Fancy fainting like that. How mortifying. And poor Sam having to carry her.

Sam got in the driver's side, turned in his seat, and said, "Don't faint again, but I'm going to tell you something which might shock you even more."

She took another drink of water. "Go on."

"Not everyone who works for the police is honest."

Maggie blinked at that statement. She didn't know what to say.

Sam went on. "I do a lot of work for security companies, and sometimes, I work with the police. I know how easy it is to break into their computer systems. I've even shown them how easy it is. It doesn't matter how often they improve it, if someone's determined to hack it, then they will. Are you surprised?"

"Not really. I watch crime shows. I know what goes on."

Sam gave her a wry smile. "You don't know the half of it. The officers I've dealt with at this station are great. I don't suspect any of them of stealing the recording device. Or of deleting the details of your report."

Maggie couldn't help saying, "Not even your ex-wife?"

"Not even her. But it could be someone else. Someone who's new to the station. Or someone who's been there a while. Even a temp, or a cleaner, or..."

He trailed off, and shrugged. "What I'm trying to say is that it's not a safe place. The person who killed your neighbour is more organised than I first thought."

"What do you mean?"

"I thought it could have been a passion killing, you know, done in the heat of the moment. But it doesn't look that way now. The killer could have set up an alert for any reporting of the crime."

Maggie's eyes widened. "They can do that?"

"They can. If that's the case, they've got your details, and they know what the footage shows."

Maggie slumped in the seat. "And they deleted the crime from the police computer and stole the box. And they know I saw the footage too."

"Exactly. But I can do something about this. I have contacts who can help. I will—" His face turned ashen. "Oh no. What an idiot I am!" He suddenly shifted in his seat, switched the engine on, and drove away at speed.

Maggie held on to the handle of the door. "Whoa! Slow down! We're in the middle of town. What's wrong?"

Sam gripped the steering wheel tightly. "I put a copy of the footage on my computer earlier. I've left a virtual trail of the crime. Someone could have seen me at the police station with you. I'm known amongst the criminal elements around here. And not for good reasons. Someone could have accessed my computer remotely." He swerved around a corner, narrowly missing an elderly man crossing the road. Sam mouthed an apology at the man. The man made an obscene gesture in response.

"Sam, please slow down. You're going to crash. What about that sweeping thing you did at the office? Doesn't that protect your computer too? You work in security. Could your computer really be accessed remotely?"

"It never has been, but it could. It depends who we're dealing with. Nowhere is safe. Not even my shop."

A siren blasted out from behind them. Sam pulled over to the side to let a fire engine go past.

Maggie watched it race along the road. She said, "I've never seen a fire engine in the middle of Leeds before. I wonder where it's going?"

Sam suddenly sped off after the fire engine. His knuckles were white.

"Sam! Slow down!"

"My shop. The fire engine is heading towards my shop."

"No. It can't be." Maggie stared in bewilderment as the fire engine did indeed head in the direction of Sam's shop. "But...you don't think..." She couldn't get the words out.

He flashed her a quick look, his eyes full of worry. "That someone has set my shop on fire? Yes, I do think that."

"Oh! That young man will be in there. The one who works for you. What's his name again?"

"Jake. He's not just my employee. He's my son."

Chapter 14

"Your son? Why didn't you tell me that earlier?"

"It didn't come up." Sam decreased his speed as the traffic slowed in front of them. He lowered his window, stuck his head out, and yelled, "Move! This is an emergency!"

The traffic didn't move.

Maggie's blood ran cold. "Can you smell smoke?"

Sam nodded, his face grey. He yelled again at the cars in front of him.

"Shouting at them won't make any difference," Maggie said, and immediately regretted it. "Sorry. That's not helpful at all. Look, why don't you get out and run to your shop? It's not far. I'll park your van somewhere. There's a car park up there on the left."

"Thanks." Sam shot her a quick smile, then opened the door and ran off down a side street.

Of course, the traffic started to move at that second. Horns blasted out behind the stationary white van.

"Hang on!" Maggie shouted back at the noise. With no dignity whatsoever, she clambered over to the driver's side, adjusted the seat, and set off. She glanced to the side and saw Sam's disappearing back as he rounded a corner.

"Please let his son be okay. Please. Please," Maggie muttered to herself as she drove into the nearest car park. It was a multi-storey one, and she had to drive to the top before she found a space. Trying to quell her rising panic, she parked up, located the ticket machine, and then rushed out of the car park.

As she raced towards Sam's shop, she silently berated herself. This was all her fault. Why did she have to record those hedgehogs? It was none of her business what they did. And so what if her neighbours thought she was making it up about having the hedgehogs in her garden? Why did she have to prove she wasn't lying? Why did she care so much what others thought of her? Look where it had got her.

The sensible side of her brain tried to point out a murder had occurred on her street, and that the murderer couldn't be allowed to get away with it.

She told the sensible part of her brain to shut up, and continued making her way to Ward's Surveillance Supplies.

Maggie vaguely became aware of the smoke not smelling as strongly now. Had the fire been put out? Was Jake okay? Was the shop still in one piece?

As soon as she walked around the corner, she found out the answers to all of her questions.

Chapter 15

The shop was okay. There was no evidence of any fire which had taken place. The door was ajar, and as Maggie got closer, she saw Sam's arms wrapped around his son. Jake was giving his dad a one-armed hug because he was holding a large brown bag in the other.

She rushed into the shop, and for a moment, was tempted to join in with the hug. She resisted. She said, "You're okay. And your shop is okay."

Sam released Jake from his embrace and smiled over at Maggie. "The fire was in another building in the next street."

"I hope they're okay," Maggie said.

Jake spoke, "They are. I walked past it on the way here." He frowned at Maggie. "Why are you here again? I thought you'd taken that device to the police?"

Maggie opened her mouth to explain, but Sam held his hand up to silence her. He made a couple of hand gestures to Jake, who appeared to understand every one because he swiftly put his bag down, and took his phone out. Sam did the same, and they did something on their phones for the next few minutes while Maggie waited silently.

Sam put his phone away, and said, "We're safe. Jake, why did you leave the shop? I told you to never leave it without informing me."

Jake picked the brown bag up. "But I had to. It's your fault. You should have got them to deliver like you normally do."

"What are you going on about?"

"My dinner. The takeaway down the road called me. They said you'd ordered some food and paid for it. But I had to collect it because they said you'd refused to pay the delivery charge. Why didn't you pay it? I had to walk all the way down to the shop, and back again."

"I didn't order your dinner," Sam replied quietly. "What time was this?"

Jake gave a half-shrug, "About thirty minutes ago. It's hot food, so I had to collect it."

Sam gave him an intense look. "And you checked every door was locked before you left?"

"Of course I did!" Jake's belligerent tone swiftly changed as realisation dawned. "Oh. It wasn't you who ordered it, was it?"

Sam shook his head, and then looked around the premise. "The front door was locked. I can't see any signs of forced entry. Nothing seems to be missing from the cabinets." His attention landed on the desk at the rear of the room. He strode over to it and stopped in front of the computer he'd been on earlier. His face fell.

Maggie went over to him. "What's wrong?"

"Someone's been on my computer." He gave Jake a half-hopeful look. "Was it you?"

"No," Jake said. He moved closer to Sam. "Have they deleted anything?"

Sam sat down and started pressing the keys on the keyboard. After a minute, he let out a sigh, sat back in his chair, and said, "They've accessed your footage, Maggie. They've deleted it. Probably after taking a copy. I've checked the backups we have, but they've deleted those too. The CCTV has been wiped. The person who's done this is very tech-savvy. And they know how to break into a premise without leaving any evidence."

Jake said, "And they know what I like eating. Fried chicken burger with salt-and-pepper fries. How would they know that?"

Sam gave him a resigned look. "Don't you put pictures of food on your social media accounts? I've warned you about that."

"It's just pictures of food." Jake defended himself. "I don't put anything about my personal life online."

Sam continued to look at him.

Jake's head dropped, and he put the food bag on the desk. "Sorry, Dad. I'll delete my social profiles. All of them. Sorry."

Sam gave him a kind look. "I know how difficult this job is for you, but it's safety first. Always." He turned back to the computer. "I don't know what to do now. That footage was all we had."

Maggie suddenly had a thought. She retrieved her phone from her handbag. "Hang on. I think I might have something on here. I connected the recording device to my phone when I bought it. The footage might be on my phone. I didn't even think to look there. Ah, here's the icon for the device."

Before she could tap on the icon, Jake snatched the phone from her hands, threw it to the floor and stamped on it.

Maggie stared in horror at her shattered phone. "Why did you do that?"

Chapter 16

"I had to do it," Jake said. He lifted his chin as if daring Maggie to argue with him.

Maggie did argue with him. "You did NOT have to do that! How dare you? I've got everything on that phone! All my contacts. All my reminders. And now look at it!"

Jake took a step back. "You were about to give your position away. If you haven't already." He cast an imploring look Sam's way. "Tell her. I had to do it."

"You did not!" Maggie cried out. "I could have switched it off. You vandal!"

Sam stood up and put himself between Maggie and Jake. He looked uncertain as to whom he should talk to first. "Jake, I know you thought you were doing the right thing, but you didn't have to destroy Maggie's phone." He aimed a smile at Maggie. "Jake was only trying to protect you. If you'd have clicked on the footage, you would have given yourself away to whoever has the recording device."

"Wouldn't they know anyway?" Maggie argued. "If they have the device, won't they be able to see what it's linked to?" She glowered at Jake to let him know he wasn't forgiven.

Sam explained, "Possibly, but sometimes those devices are only activated once a phone connects to the footage which has been recorded."

Maggie still hadn't given up her arguing her point. "But if the killer already has the police report, they'll know who I am, and where I live, and how old I am. Not that my age is anyone's business."

"Wait," Jake said. "What are you talking about? And I don't mean your age."

Sam told him about the missing police report and the stolen recording device.

Jake turned pale. He opened the food bag, took a handful of fries out and shoved them in his mouth. He chewed them for a bit, swallowed, and said, "We're dealing with a criminal mastermind who won't rest until they've destroyed all evidence of their crime. And that includes us." He took another handful of fries and pushed them into his mouth.

Maggie's mothering instinct came out. She put her hand on Jake's shoulder, and said, "I'm sure the police will help us. They know about the crime now. Don't eat so quickly. You'll give yourself a stomach ache." She was tempted to push the floppy hair off his face but stopped herself in time.

Hope alighted in Jake's eyes. "I'll phone Mum! Of course. She'll help us. Or me anyway. I'll give her a ring right now."

Sam said, "I'm not sure about that. She'll think I put you up to it. And she'll be annoyed that you're involved. Jake, did you watch Maggie's footage?"

"Of course I did. As soon as you two left for the station." He took his phone out, looked at it, and then handed it to Sam. "Time for a phone swap?"

Sam pulled a key from his pocket, and then pushed back his chair. Maggie watched in amazement as he pulled part of the carpet back to reveal a small trapdoor in the wooden floor. Sam used the key to open the trapdoor. There was a safe beneath it. He keyed a long series of numbers into the pad, opened the safe, and reached inside. It was full of phones, documents, metal boxes, and other things which Maggie couldn't identify because Sam quickly closed the safe.

"Here you are," he said as he handed a phone to Jake. He then gave a phone to Maggie. "This is a safe phone. No one can track you on this. Do you know the telephone numbers of all your contacts? If you don't, there is a way I can get your details. Don't ask me how."

Maggie took the phone. "I always make a list of phone numbers in my diary. Call me old-fashioned, but I like to write things down in a physical book. I've got all my appointments written down too." She gave Jake a sheepish smile. "Sorry for shouting at you."

"That's all right," Jake said with a small smile. "I'll phone Mum." He went into the side room.

Maggie looked at the remnants of her phone, and said, "Shall I clean this up? Have you got a dustpan and brush somewhere?"

"I'll do it." Sam gave her a long look which made Maggie feel a bit unsettled. He said, "I'm so sorry you're involved in this."

She let out a short laugh. "I got myself involved. I'm sorry I dragged you into it. And your son."

"We've been dragged into worse things. All is not lost. There are still things I can do. But your safety is my priority. I know we've only known each other for a short time, but I don't want you to be in any danger."

Maggie looked at her feet, suddenly finding them very interesting. She mumbled, "I'll be fine."

Sam said, "I've got a suggestion."

Maggie looked back at him. "Oh?"

She didn't find out what his suggestion was because Jake burst into the room with a huge smile on his face. He declared, "It's all right! Everything's okay. Mum's sorted it out."

Sam's eyes narrowed. "What has she done now?"

Chapter 17

Still smiling, Jake explained, "I told Mum that I'd seen the footage too, and what was on it. She said she'd sort everything out. And she said you're not to get involved any further." He gave Sam a pointed look. Jake then looked at Maggie. "She said you don't need to worry because the police will deal with everything now, and that you don't have to bother my dad anymore."

Maggie raised one eyebrow in Sam's direction. She didn't like being told what to do, and going by the stony expression on Sam's face, neither did he.

Sam's voice belied the look in his eyes. In a casual tone, he said, "Did your mother say what she was going to do? And how she was going to sort things out?"

Jake moved over to the desk and perched on the edge of it. He reached into the paper bag and pulled out a burger. "Yeah, she told me what she's going to do." He took a huge bite of the burger.

"And?" Sam prompted him. "What is she going to do?"

With his cheeks bulging with food, Jake said, "She's going to send a couple of officers around to that house where the murder took place." He pulled a look of disgust. "This burger is nearly cold." He took another bite anyway.

Maggie was less patient than Sam. "Is that it?" she asked. "She's going to send a couple of officers there? When? This is an urgent matter, you know. Someone has been murdered. Right on my street."

Jake's look became evasive. "Well, we don't know that for certain. It looked like a murder, but Mum said it could have been someone messing about. She even said you—" He abruptly stopped, blushed, and stood up. "I've got stuff to do." He turned away.

"Stop right there," Sam demanded. "What did your mum say about Maggie?"

Jake picked at something in his burger, and muttered, "She said Maggie could have made the footage herself, maybe from a video online."

"Why on earth would I do that?" Maggie asked.

"Mum said you wanted some attention because you're probably bored and lonely."

Maggie was too stunned to speak.

Sam wasn't. "That was a malicious thing for your mother to say. She should know better. Jake, you can do some work in the other room. Get in touch with some of our contacts about the deleted footage on my computer. See if there's a way to retrieve it, or if there's a copy on the dark web."

"But Mum said—"

"I know what your mum said. She can do her job, and I'll do mine." He looked at Maggie. "If you would like my help, that is?"

Maggie merely nodded. Did Sam think she was bored and lonely too? Did he feel sorry for her? She cleared her throat, and asked, "Do you think the footage is genuine, Sam?"

"I certainly do."

She looked at Jake. "What about you?"

He shrugged in reply. "It looked genuine enough. But fakes nearly always do." He shrugged again. "Can I go now?" His question was directed at Sam, who gave him a curt nod. Jake disappeared into the other room.

Sam said to Maggie, "You'll have to forgive his rudeness. He idolizes his mum and believes everything she says. Despite the things she's done."

"What has she done?" Maggie asked. Then she shook her head. "Sorry, it's none of my business. Unless you want to talk about it?"

"I don't. Where have you parked the van?"

Maggie told him where, and then handed over the keys and the parking voucher.

He said, "Thanks for doing that. I really did think my shop was on fire."

"So did I. Do you often get into dangerous situations?"

Sam nodded. "It comes with the job. I never wanted Jake to work with me, but he wouldn't take no for an answer. Even his mum couldn't talk him out of it. She claims I brainwashed him into working here. She's always trying to get him to leave. Sometimes, I wish he would. He's seen and heard far too many disturbing things." He sighed. "Why can't we ever let our children grow up?"

"Because we love them. We want to protect them from the world. But it's impossible. I've tried." Maggie gave him a small smile. "Thanks for helping me. What should we do next?"

Sam pointed to his computer. "I've got some enquiries to make. Once I've gone through a thorough security check, of course. The person who deleted the footage knew what they were doing, and they could have planted a tracking device anywhere in the shop."

"Don't you have a stash of other computers hidden under the floorboards?" Maggie looked around her as if expecting to see laptops popping up through the carpet.

Sam replied, "I do have other devices I can use, but for your safety, I won't tell you where they are."

Maggie laughed. Then she stopped when she saw how serious he was. "What do you mean?"

"I'd rather not say."

"I'd rather you did." She gave him an intense look.

"Well, if someone questioned you at a later date about my business, I wouldn't want you to tell them where I keep sensitive information. I shouldn't have shown you where I kept my phones. I'll have to move them now."

Maggie slowly shook her head. "I don't know whether you're lying or not. Why would I tell anyone where you keep things?"

From the other room, Jake helpfully shouted, "You might get tortured until you admit the truth. Maggie, Mum said there are some police cars on your street now, and it's safe for you to go home."

Maggie still didn't like being told what to do, but the thought of going home and away from this strange environment suddenly appealed to her. Perhaps the police would be better at dealing with this rather than Sam and his son.

She said to Sam, "I will go home. I'll let you know what the police find out. If they do find anything out. And if they actually tell me. I suppose your ex-wife will let Jake know before me anyway."

"Maggie, I don't think you should go home," Sam said.

"Where do you suggest I go? Stay here?"

"You could."

She sighed heavily. "I want to go home. I feel safe at home. And the police are on my street. I'll be fine."

"I'll give you a lift," Sam offered.

"No, I'd rather get the bus. Thanks."

Before he could say another word, Maggie left the shop. She heard him say, "I'll be in touch on that phone I've given you." She didn't reply.

On the bus home, she leaned her head against the window and tried to make sense of everything. But she couldn't make sense of any of it. Why was this happening to her?

She felt marginally better when she walked along her street a short while later. There were three police cars parked there, and some uniformed officers were talking to various neighbours. Good. Something was being done. Maggie didn't have to worry any longer.

Or so she thought.

Chapter 18

The police came to call on Maggie later. She invited them into her house, and then explained why she'd set the recording device up in the first place. The police officers remained polite throughout the interview, and Maggie couldn't tell whether they believed her or not. In desperation, she took them into the back garden and showed them where the hedgehogs lived. Of course, the hedgehogs refused to show themselves.

Maggie asked them if they'd spoken to the present occupant in number forty-eight, but they refused to give her any information on that. Which was a bit unreasonable, she thought, considering how it was Maggie who'd recorded the crime. But she didn't say that, though.

The police stayed a bit longer on the street, and Maggie began to feel a tad safer. Sam didn't get in touch, and she told herself that was a good thing. Wasn't it?

She sent a text message to her son and said she was using a temporary phone because she'd lost hers. She had thought Oscar would become suspicious at the text because she wasn't someone who lost things. She was someone who knew where everything was. Like most mothers.

But Oscar hadn't questioned her about the temporary phone when he sent a reply text. He had asked her if Carmella had returned home unexpectedly. He was becoming obsessed with her attractive neighbour. She'd have to keep an eye on that situation.

The police left a few hours later, but to Maggie's relief, one of the cars stayed parked up at the end of the street. She hoped they would stay there all night.

Maggie took a long bath with the expensive bubble bath Carmella had bought her for Christmas. It had lots of essential oils which were supposed to relax a person. And Maggie did start to relax. The essential oils really helped. And so did the glass of wine at her side.

She felt much better after the bath, and settled down in front of the TV and watched a movie. A comedy, not a scary one. She didn't need any more scares in her life at the moment.

Chapter 19

The killer placed a gloved hand against the outside of Maggie's living room window and looked through the gap in the curtains.

The killer smiled.

Look at her. Sitting there in her pyjamas, sipping wine and laughing at that terrible movie. Not a care in the world. Poor, deluded woman. She would have to die, of course.

The killer was sorry about that. But it had to be done. And soon.

The killer's smile grew. Perhaps they could have a bit of fun with the deluded woman first.

Chapter 20

Despite the funny movie and the glasses of wine, Maggie didn't sleep well that night. She kept dreaming about giant hedgehogs chasing her down the street and into the arms of a shadowy person. And then the shadowy person produced a knife out of nowhere and began to chase Maggie straight back to the enormous hedgehogs. As soon as one dream ended, another hedgehog one began as if on a loop.

"This is just silly," Maggie said to herself as she got up at 6 a.m. "I can't keep having dreams like this. And now I'm talking to myself."

She checked the unfamiliar phone at her side and was relieved that there weren't any messages from Sam. Which only meant one thing: the police had everything firmly in hand. Right?

There was a message from Oscar to say he would be out of his office all day, and not to worry if he didn't get in touch as he would be in meetings with important clients. She smiled. He so loved his job. Ever since he was a boy, he'd always wanted to save the planet from pollution and other factors, and now his job allowed him to do that. At least, as much as one person could do to help the planet. She was very proud of him.

Maggie got dressed and then headed to the kitchen. She switched the radio on and opened the kitchen curtains. The sight of the clear, blue sky cheered her immensely. She would put a wash on and then hang it out. She laughed at her thoughts. When did a sunny day immediately equate to getting her washing hung out? Was it an age thing? She could take herself off for the day instead. Go to the seaside. Sit on the beach and eat a huge ice cream. Take a long walk on the promenade. She had the whole day to herself.

Maggie considered her options. And then put a load of clothes in the washing machine anyway. She wasn't the type to just take herself off on a whim. She used to do when she was younger, but she didn't do that sort of thing now. Anyway, she had a delivery due from Amazon at some point. It might come today. She wanted to be at home for that.

Maggie put the kettle on and prepared her breakfast. The washing machine whirred quietly. Once she'd made a cup of tea, she sat at the kitchen table and made a list of everything she needed to do that week. It was only June, but she wondered if she should start on her Christmas plans. It was never too early to start on that. There was always so much to do.

She kept herself busy with her list, and successfully put all thoughts of yesterday's events right out of her mind.

But, eventually, her mind began to wander. Had the police got any further with their enquiries? Had they spoken to that bad-tempered woman who claimed she lived at number forty-eight now? She had told the police about her talk with the elderly woman, but they didn't even make a note of her conversation.

The washing machine beeped and pulled Maggie out of her thoughts. She'd let the police do their job. She had enough things to keep her busy without worrying about her neighbours.

Maggie hung the washing out. She heard a rustling coming from the bushes at her side. A little nose peeped out. It was one of the hedgehogs.

Maggie pointed to it, and said, "This is all your fault. Coming into my garden and causing disruptions. You're nothing but trouble."

The creature shuffled a bit further out of the bushes and appeared to be listening to her every word.

Maggie's heart softened. How could she be mad at such a beautiful animal?

She moved over to it, knelt on the grass, and said, "You're not supposed to be out in the day. You're nocturnal. Did you know that? Go on; get yourself back in the bushes and go to sleep."

The hedgehog's nose twitched as if it were waiting for her to say something else.

Maggie smiled at it. "Do you need more food? I've got some dog food in the kitchen. I'll bring a tin out for you. But it's not to eat now. It's for nighttime. The time when you're supposed to be awake. Okay?"

The hedgehog seemed happy with that suggestion and shuffled back into the bushes.

Maggie straightened up. Should she be concerned that she was now talking to hedgehogs? Nope. But she would become concerned if they started talking back.

She walked towards the kitchen door. What was that on the doorstep?

She moved closer and picked the item up. It was an ornament in the shape of a hedgehog. The hedgehog was wearing two pairs of yellow boots.

Where had it come from? Had it been there when she'd taken her washing out earlier? She hadn't noticed it.

Had Sam left it there? If so, why? Or maybe it was Jake who'd wanted to apologise for his mother's cruel words about her.

Maggie didn't know what to make of the ornament. She didn't know where it had come from. But it was cute. She'd put it on a shelf somewhere.

She went into the kitchen and put the ornament on the table for now. She'd better put that food out for the hedgehogs before she forgot. She had a nice collection of small tins of dog food in her cupboard. When she'd first seen the little creatures in her garden, she'd done a thorough internet search of what a person should do when they find hedgehogs in their garden. The main message was to leave them alone, but you could put water and dog food out for them. Which Maggie had done on a regular basis.

She took the nearest tin out of the cupboard, ripped the lid off and returned to the garden. Once the food was in place, she went back to the kitchen and looked at the hedgehog ornament again.

She turned it over in her hands. Oh, what was that? There was a small, rolled-up piece of paper stuck to the bottom of the ornament. A message? Or a manufacturer's note about where the ornament had been made?

Maggie carefully peeled the paper off. With a bit of difficulty, she unrolled it.

Something had been printed on the paper in tiny words. Maggie couldn't make the words out.

She put her reading glasses on, and read it again.

She gasped. Then dropped the note in shock. Picked it up, and read it again:

'Dear Maggie, I know what you saw. I'm coming to get you next. The police can't help you now.'

Chapter 21

Maggie was still shaking as she walked into Ward's Surveillance Supplies thirty minutes later.

Sam instantly took in her pale face and jumped to his feet. He rushed over to her side. "Maggie, what's wrong? You're trembling. Have you seen another murder?"

Maggie couldn't speak. She felt sick to her stomach with fear.

Sam guided her over to the desk and into one of the chairs behind it. He opened a drawer and took out a water bottle. He twisted the lid off and handed it to her. "Take some slow sips. I've got something stronger if you need it."

Maggie's hands trembled as she drank a fair bit of the water. Some dribbled down her chin, and she quickly wiped it away.

Sam waited patiently for her to speak. But she still couldn't talk for the fear lodged in her throat. So, she pulled the hedgehog ornament from her bag and gave it to Sam.

He gave her a quizzical look.

After another drink of water, Maggie said, "This was on my doorstep. I don't know how long it had been there, or where it came from. But this was attached to the bottom of it." She gave him the note.

Sam's eyes widened when he read it. He gave Maggie a long look. She was surprised to see such worry there. He said, "Did you hear anyone outside your house last night or this morning?"

"No, I don't think so. But I had the TV on last night, and the radio on this morning." She looked at the ornament. "Do you think the killer put it there? Do you think they're serious about coming for me? What does that even mean? Do they intend to kill me too?" She began to tremble again, and the bottle slipped from her hands.

Sam swiftly caught the bottle in one hand and placed it on the table. He put the ornament on the table too. Then he took Maggie's hands in his. She felt comforted by the warmth in his hands.

He said, "I haven't heard back from the police, despite phoning them several times. Were they still at your house when you got home yesterday?"

Maggie nodded, and then told him about her interview with the police. She ended with, "There was a police car on the street last night, but it wasn't there this morning. Should I take this ornament and note to the police? I wasn't sure what to do. So, I came here. I thought you could help."

"I'm glad you came here."

"Has Jake heard anything from his mum?"

"No, I asked him that this morning when he came in. We don't live in the same house anymore. I think working with me all day is more than enough for Jake. He's in the back room at the moment. I'll ask him again." Sam yelled out Jake's name causing Maggie to jump.

Jake strolled into the room with a half-eaten sausage roll in his hand. Maggie noticed flakes of pastry stuck in his beard.

"Yeah? What is it?" Jake asked. He saw Maggie, and nodded at her whilst aiming the sausage roll towards his mouth.

Sam asked, "Have you heard from your mother this morning?"

Jake rolled his eyes. "No. And stop asking me about that. Mum knows how to do her job. If she's got anything to tell me, then she'll get in touch." He took an impossibly large bite of the roll.

Sam beckoned him over. He released Maggie's hands and pointed to the ornament and note. "Look at these. They were left outside Maggie's house."

Jake ambled over and looked at the items. A few pastry flakes dropped onto the ornament.

Sam admonished him. "Be careful. This is evidence. Maggie has been threatened."

Jake gave Maggie a strange look. It was a look which made Maggie instantly alert. She suspected Jake had heard back from his mum. And he hadn't told his dad about it.

She said firmly, "Jake, what did your mum say?"

He looked at his roll. "She hasn't said anything to me."

"Jake, look at me," Maggie said. She had seen that guilty look on her son's face many times over the years. "Jake, look at me now, please."

He reluctantly did so. Maggie didn't say anything but gave him the look which she used on Oscar to get him to tell her the truth.

It worked on Jake. Spots of colour appeared on his cheeks. He shifted from foot to foot. "I don't want to tell you."

"Jake," Sam said sternly, "tell us what your mum said."

Jake was jigging about so much now, that Maggie thought he might break into a dance. Bits of sausage roll were floating to the ground like flaky snow.

Maggie gently took the roll from Jake, and said kindly, "You can tell me anything. If it's about me, and what happened on my street, don't you think I deserve to know?"

Jake's nod was almost imperceptible. He blurted out, "Mum thinks you're making it up. The police spoke to everyone on your street, and they all said they never saw that Scottish man in number forty-eight. And they said you're always staring out of your window and looking at the neighbours. They said you don't have a life, and so you spy on everyone else to see what they're doing. They said you're sad because your husband died, and your son left home, and now you've got nothing in your life."

Sam held his hand up. "That's enough, Jake."

But like a torrent of water crashing down a hill, Jake hadn't finished yet. "Some of your neighbours have seen you talking to yourself. They think you're mad."

Maggie tipped her head to one side. She did talk to herself sometimes, but only when she thought she was alone.

"And Mum thinks you made everything up so you could have lots of attention because you've got a sad life with nothing going on. She said wanting attention all the time is a medical condition, but I can't remember the name of it." He finally ran out of steam and stopped talking. He gave Maggie a look which seemed full of pity.

Maggie didn't appreciate that look one little bit. She handed the roll back to Jake, and said, "Did your mum say anything about the investigation? Are the police making further enquiries?"

Jake slowly shook his head. "She said there's no evidence, and the footage could be false." He glanced at the ornament. "I suppose you could take that to her, and see what she says."

"There's no point. I know what she'd say," Maggie replied sadly.

Sam had been silent throughout Jake's gush of words. But he spoke now. "We will take this evidence to the police. Once I've taken photos first. We will make sure it is logged onto their system. We'll get a case number. I'll make sure of that too. Whether they believe us or not is up to them. But I want to make this latest development official."

The use of the word "us" bolstered Maggie's spirits. At least Sam still believed her. She wasn't sure why he did, but it brought her some comfort.

She said, "And then what? I've got a feeling there's something else on your mind."

Sam gave her a smile full of confidence. "Once we've been to the station, we will make our own investigations."

"We will?"

"We will. I've dealt with many hopeless cases before."

"Hopeless cases?" Maggie's spirits deflated. "You think I'm hopeless?"

Sam was immediately contrite. "No, of course not. I meant, you know, because the police don't believe you." He looked at Jake. "I don't want you telling your mum about this."

"But what if she asks me? I can't lie to her. And you shouldn't ask me to lie."

"No. Sorry. I didn't mean that. If she asks, tell her whatever you want to. I'm going to help Maggie get to the bottom of this."

"Do you want my help?" Jake asked half-heartedly.

"No. It's better if you keep out of it. But thanks for that info you obtained yesterday."

"What info?" Maggie asked.

Sam said, "We put a trace on the people who've lived at number forty-eight Lilac Lane over the years. Someone's looking into it as we speak. I'm not sure we'll get anywhere, but it's a start." He stood up. "Let's go to the station now. Ready?"

"Ready." Maggie stood up.

Jake shook his head at them both, and then took himself and his sausage roll into the side room.

As they walked out of the shop, Maggie said nervously, "Erm, you know yesterday, you told me not to make any investigations of my own."

Sam nodded. "Yes, I remember."

"I called at number forty-eight and spoke to an angry woman."

Sam smiled. "I would have gone to the house too. Tell me what the angry woman said on the way to the station."

Chapter 22

Sam listened without interrupting as they walked through the streets of Leeds. When Maggie had finished talking, he asked, "So, you've never seen that woman before?"

"No."

"And she claims she's lived there for a while?"

"She didn't exactly say that, but I would have seen her if she had." Maggie broke into a smile. "With me being a nosy neighbour and all that. I would have seen her during the many hours I stand at my window spying on my neighbours. Spying on them while I thought about how sad and lonely my life is." There was a spark of truth in the latter statement, but Maggie chose to ignore it.

Sam laughed. "Yes, you would have seen her. I wonder why your neighbours said that about you? Have you upset them?"

"Not at all! I'm a lovely neighbour. I'm always doing favours for them. And when Vera, who lives three doors down, broke her leg last summer, I mowed her lawn every other week. I still do it now and again for her if she's not up to it. And if anyone forgets to take their bins out, I'll do it for them too. And if it rains while Joseph's washing is out — he lives next door — I'll take his washing in." She came to a sudden stop as she realised what she was saying. "I spend far too much time at home, don't I?"

Sam gave her a kind smile. "What you do with your time is your business. Your neighbours might not have said that about you. My ex-wife is good at twisting the truth to satisfy her own needs."

"But why would she do that?"

"She's got a malicious streak, but for Jake's sake, I have to stay in contact with her. Don't pay any attention to her. Let's keep walking."

They proceeded along the street.

Maggie pointed out, "I have to pay attention to her. I suppose I'll have a police record now. For being a liar, and someone who talks to herself all the time."

"Talking to yourself is not a crime. I do it too. It's the only time I have an intelligent conversation."

Maggie laughed at that.

As they neared the police station, Sam said, "I'm sorry to hear about your husband dying. Was it recently?"

"Fourteen years ago. Oscar was ten at the time." Maggie's voice got caught in her throat. "I know I should be over it by now, but I'm not. But at least I'm getting on with my life and keeping myself busy."

Sam added gently. "I don't understand it when people say you should be over someone's death by a certain point. Grief doesn't have an expiry date."

"You're right about that." She hoped he wouldn't ask her any more questions about Harry. She was okay most of the time, but for some reason, today was a difficult day. She really could have done with Harry at her side. She glanced at Sam as they walked into the police station. Having Sam as a substitute wasn't that bad. And he was easy on the eyes too.

Maggie almost jumped at that thought. Where had that come from? She was in the middle of a very serious situation. She shouldn't be thinking about how handsome Sam was. Pull yourself together woman!

Sam suddenly looked her way. He frowned, and said, "Are you okay? You look flushed. Are you too hot?"

"No, not at all," Maggie blustered. "No hot flashes for me! Not since I started using those marvellous HRT patches!"

Sam blinked. "Right. Okay." He walked ahead of her.

Maggie's head dropped. Why had she said that? Of all things! She looked over her shoulder at the exit door. She could make a run for it. And keep on running until she was as far away from Sam as possible.

Sam tapped her on the shoulder. She looked at him. He said quietly, "Would you let me make the report? I don't want anyone messing you about."

Relief rushed through Maggie. It was followed by a spark of indignation. She could take care of herself.

As if reading her mind, Sam continued, "I know you can do this yourself, but I'd like to do it. And, fair warning, I'm going to use my outside voice. There could be a few curse words thrown in too." He grinned. "You might want to cover your ears for that."

Maggie didn't know what to say. As she looked into his brown eyes, she felt a flutter of something in her stomach. It was such an unfamiliar feeling that she couldn't give it a name. Why was he doing this for her?

She said, "Yes, please. Thank you."

"It's my pleasure," he said. "Let the show begin."

Chapter 23

And it was a show.

Sam marched up to the reception desk, banged his fist on it, and shouted at the young man behind it. "I want to see DCI Dexter right now! I know he's here. I saw his car outside."

Maggie stood a little way back. Who was DCI Dexter? She soon found out as a man about her age came walking through a door at the side. He was tall and well-built, with a full head of dark hair. There was a certain handsomeness about him, but it was offset by the arrogant way he walked, and the smug smile which flittered across his face when he saw Sam.

"Sam," DCI Dexter announced as he walked over to the desk and stood behind it. "What an absolute pleasure to see you. Do you want to come through to my office? I'll get the whisky out. We'll have a catch-up. I spoke to your Jake last week. He's getting taller every day, isn't he? I'm not sure about that beard of his. But they all have them these days. Come through." He turned to the side as if fully expecting Sam to follow him.

Sam didn't. "I'm not here for a catch-up. I'm here to report a serious crime. Can you take the details down, if it's not beneath you?"

The young police officer's eyebrows rose so much that they nearly left his face. He took a step away from DCI Dexter.

Maggie took a step closer. This was an interesting conversation. How did these two know each other?

"A serious crime?" DCI Dexter repeated. He glanced towards Maggie, and his look lingered too long. He looked back at Sam. "Is it something to do with that hedgehog fiasco? And that fake footage? I heard about that. We've had a good laugh about it." He looked at Maggie again with a definite sneer on his face.

Maggie's blood began to boil. Blooming cheek. Who does he think he is?

Sam slapped his hand heavily on the desk again. "How dare you! That footage wasn't fake at all. I can vouch for that. And for you to say you've all had a laugh about it! Do you mean the whole station? Is that how you treat citizens around here? Shame on you. When this is over, I'll be making an official complaint."

DCI Dexter held his hands up in defence. "Calm down. What are you getting so upset about?"

"What am I getting so upset about?" Sam's voice rose. "I'll tell you what I'm getting upset about, you—"

Maggie winced at the words which came out of Sam's mouth. Wow, he knew some colourful expressions.

DCI Dexter's expression hardened under the onslaught, but he didn't say anything.

Sam took a deep breath and attempted to calm himself down. Maggie had no idea whether this was still part of his act or not. Sam said, "And now there is new evidence to add to the previous crime. I want you to record this immediately, and to give me a crime number."

"I can't give you a crime number unless I know it is a crime," DCI Dexter retorted.

That was the wrong thing to say. Sam proceeded to DCI Dexter a piece of his mind. The young police officer behind the desk discreetly walked away and into the safety of the room beyond.

Sam ended his outburst with, "You will record this as a crime. And you'll do it now. If you don't, I will take this matter higher immediately. I know my rights inside and out. I would also like a copy of the report for this crime, and for you to note it is linked to the footage taken by Ms Kelburn."

DCI Dexter's eyes were full of hate. So was his voice. "I shall give it to Ms Kelburn seeing as it's none of your business."

"It is my business," Sam told him. "Ms Kelburn is my client."

His client? Maggie tried not to show her surprise. Since when? And was she supposed to pay him?

Sam looked over his shoulder, gave her a quick wink which DCI Dexter didn't see, and said, "Isn't that right, Ms Kelburn?"

Ah, it was part of his act. Hopefully.

Maggie addressed DCI Dexter. "Mr Ward is correct. You can give a copy of the report to Mr Ward. And I'll have a copy too. Thank you."

"Of course," the inspector replied coldly. He moved over a little bit. "Give me a moment while I sign into this screen, and then I'll take the details of this new crime." He almost spat the last word out.

Sam seemed to take great pleasure in reporting the ornament incident to DCI Dexter. He even made the inspector repeat all the information back a few times to make sure it had been recorded properly. Maggie would have felt sorry for the inspector if he hadn't been so awful to them. She wondered again how the two men knew each other.

It didn't take her long to find out.

Chapter 24

Maggie didn't speak until they left the police station.

"I know I'm stating the obvious, but wow, you don't like DCI Dexter. What's the history between you two? Don't tell me he's another one of your relatives? A cousin you fell out with? A brother you don't get along with? How do you know each other?"

Sam shoved his hands in his pockets, and said casually, "We used to be best friends. We met each other on the first day of school when we were four years old."

"Really?"

"Yes, really. We were best friends all through school and university. He was my best man at my wedding. And he's Jake's godfather. Do you want to stop for a bit of lunch somewhere? That café over there does great jacket potatoes."

"I'm not hungry. Is it even lunchtime?" Maggie checked her watch and was surprised to see it was nearly midday. "So, why aren't you friends now? What did he do?"

Sam flashed her a smile. "I like how you asked what he did, and not me."

"I don't like him. And I don't trust him." She shivered a little. "There's just something about him which I don't like."

"He wasn't always like that. How about fish and chips? My treat. I know the best place to get them around here."

"I'm still not hungry." Maggie had to speed up a bit to keep up with Sam's long strides. "Are you going to tell me what he did? Or do I have to guess?"

Sam pressed his lips together as if deciding whether to tell her or not.

Maggie suddenly knew what had happened. She put her hand on his elbow, causing him to stop walking. She said quietly, "He betrayed you, didn't he? With your wife."

"Ex-wife. Yep. What a cliché. I should have guessed. They always flirted with each other since the day I introduced them. I thought it was harmless. I was just pleased that Tyler got on so well with Ingrid. She's not the easiest person to get on with. As you know."

"Tyler? That's his name? It doesn't suit him."

Sam smiled briefly. "It does suit him. It rhymes with 'liar.' Tyler the liar. It's got a certain ring to it. Don't you think?" He heaved a big sigh. "Sorry. I'm being mean and bitter."

"You've every right to be. You should have let me shout at him back there too." She turned around. "Let's go back, and I'll have a go at him."

Sam laughed. "It's kind of you to offer, but we've got other things to do. Maggie, I did mean it about you being my client. But there's no way I'll charge you for my services."

"But you can't work for free."

"For free? I'm already imagining the feeling of euphoria I'll get when I prove Ingrid and Tyler wrong. I should be paying you for that."

Disappointment went through Maggie. "Is that why you're helping me? To get back at them?"

"No! Not at all. I want to help you. Very much so." His stomach rumbled. "Let's get something to eat. You might not be hungry, but I'm starving. And while we're eating, I'll tell you what can be done about the murder investigation. I've got some ideas."

Maggie relented. "Okay. But let me pay for lunch. To say thank you for helping me. And believing me."

"I can do that." He looked into her eyes causing Maggie's heart to miss a beat. "You have many questions in your eyes. I can see them. Do you want to know more about my ex-wife and ex-friend? Do you want all the gory details?"

Maggie broke into a grin. "Yes, please. And then you can tell me what we're going to do about the murder."

Sam took her to his favourite café, and after ordering a lot of food for both of them, he told her about his ex-wife and ex-friend. How they'd deceived him for years before finally admitting the truth. And how they were now living together. He tried to make light of their betrayal as he spoke, but Maggie saw the hurt in his eyes. It made her heart ache to see that.

Sam also told her about what investigations he could undertake concerning the murder. Maggie was impressed with what he proposed to do.

"And that's legal, is it?" she asked.

"Legal enough." He looked at her empty plate. "I thought you weren't hungry?"

"I didn't think I was either. But I need to keep my strength if I'm going to help you."

Sam held his hands up. "I never said you were going to help me."

"But I have to. At least a little bit. Sam, I can't sit back and do nothing. That ornament and message really scared me. I have to do something. Please. Let me help."

"I'm not sure. Let me take you home, and we'll discuss it there. I'd like to sweep your house for bugs, if that's okay with you?"

"Bugs? Really? I never thought about that. Yes, do that. Thank you."

They left the café and headed to Maggie's house in Sam's van.

Having Sam near made Maggie feel much safer.

But all feelings of safety soon vanished a short while later.

Chapter 25

Sam didn't park around the corner this time. He parked on the road in front of Maggie's house, but before Maggie could get out of the van, he said, "I'll go first."

"Why?"

"Just to make sure everything is okay," was his evasive answer. "I'll check the perimeter first." There was a steely determination in his voice, so Maggie didn't argue with him.

She watched as Sam walked towards her house. His glance went left and right. He looked ready to leap into action at any moment. He looked back at her, made some sort of signal which she didn't understand, and then walked down the path at the side of her house.

A few moments later, he returned along the path. He gave her another complicated signal before heading towards the front of the house. What did those gestures mean? Maggie wondered. Why can't he just give me a thumbs up or a thumbs down?

She shuffled forward in her seat to see what he was going to do next. This was quite entertaining.

Sam crouched and stealthily made his way along the front of the house. When he got closer to the window, he pulled a metal tube from his pocket and fiddled with it. Maggie could see the end of the tube extending upwards until it neared the bottom of the window. Was that a mini periscope? Really?

Sam looked through the periscope, if that's what it was. Then he looked over at her, his face full of confusion. What had he seen?

Maggie couldn't bear it a minute longer. She got out of the van, bent low and scurried towards him. She crouched at his side. Feeling the need to whisper, she asked, "What have you seen? Is it something scary?"

He looked at her. "Very. To me, anyway. Obviously not to you." He frowned as if seeing her for the first time. "I know you like hedgehogs, but I didn't know you were a fanatic."

"Fanatic? What do you mean?"

He pointed to the window. "All that paraphernalia you've got in there. You could open your own shop. Or wholesalers."

"What are you going on about?" Maggie stood up and looked through her window. She almost fainted when she saw what was inside. Her knees suddenly felt weak, and she grabbed on to the windowsill for support. "Those are not my things. I didn't put them there."

Sam straightened up. "You didn't?"

Maggie recovered somewhat. She jabbed her finger at the window. "I certainly did not fill my living room with those hedgehog cushions! And I did not hang those pictures of cavorting hedgehogs on my walls. And I did not put that hedgehog-shaped rug on the floor. And I—"

"I get it. You didn't put them there."

Maggie hadn't finished. "As if I'd have all those stuffed toys everywhere! You can barely see the furniture! And all those ornaments by the fireplace! Look at them all. Did you really think I would..." Her words trailed off as the horrific realisation of what she was seeing hit her. "Someone's been in my house. Someone put those things there."

Sam nodded. "They're trying to scare you."

"They're doing a good job." Maggie felt her stomach tighten in fear. "What do we do now? Shall we phone the police?"

He nodded. "You do that. I'm going to check inside. The person who did this could still be in there."

"Really?" Maggie's voice was barely audible.

"You go back to the van, and phone the police. Here, use my phone. I've recently done a security check on it."

"Will you be safe? What if there is someone inside? What if they attack you?"

He gave her a swift smile. "I can take care of myself. Can I have your keys, please? I can pick locks, but there's no point if you've got the keys."

Maggie handed him the keys, and Sam went inside via the front door. Maggie found herself unable to move. She half expected to hear yells, and cries of help coming from inside. But there was only silence.

Maggie walked halfway down the path. She didn't want to move too far away in case Sam needed her help. Not that she'd be much help, but she felt the need to be near.

She phoned the police and told them what had happened. The officer she spoke to was polite, but not very helpful. He said he'd make a note of the incident.

"Aren't you going to send someone around?" Maggie asked. "I've been broken into."

"Yes, I understand. But nothing has actually been stolen, has it? Let me just confirm what you said. Items have been left inside your house. Is that right? Items of a hedgehog nature? I'm not sure that's a crime, Ms Kelburn."

"But someone broke into my house and put them there!"

"I understand, Ms Kelburn. Please don't raise your voice or I might need to terminate our call. Is there any evidence of a break-in? Any locks damaged? Or windows smashed?"

Maggie's patience was quickly evaporating. But as calmly as she could, she said, "No, not that I can see at the moment." She was about to say Sam was inside but didn't think the officer would like that, not if the criminal was still inside.

The officer said, "I've got your details, Ms Kelburn. We'll take the appropriate action. Goodbye. Your call is appreciated."

He ended the call. Maggie stared at the phone. Were the police going to do anything? Had she imagined it, or had the officer's tone changed when she'd given her name? Perhaps she was on a police list of unreliable witnesses.

Sam came out of the house and beckoned her over. He took one look at her face, and said, "The police aren't coming here, are they?"

"It doesn't sound that way. What did you find inside?"

"Nothing. The hedgehog explosion is limited to the living room. I can't see any signs of a break-in either. If the person who did this is a professional, it's highly unlikely they left any evidence of their intrusion. Do you want to come inside and have a look? See if anything has been stolen?"

"Will you come with me?" Maggie couldn't keep up the pretence of being brave any longer. She gave him the phone back.

"Of course I will. Come on."

With Sam at her side, Maggie stepped into her house. But it didn't feel like her home. The hairs on the back of her neck lifted. The atmosphere inside felt different. Somehow hostile. Not at all comforting and welcoming like it always had been.

She went upstairs and checked the rooms there. Sam politely waited outside her bedroom because Maggie said she wanted to check her drawers in private. Thankfully, no one had been in her drawers; that was a small relief.

Once all the upstairs checks had been made, Maggie said to Sam, "Everything seems okay. I could do with a strong cup of tea. Would you like one?"

"I would. I can make it if you like? You're shaking."

Maggie let out a wobbly laugh. "I'm doing a lot of that today. I think I can manage to make a cup of tea, though."

As she headed down the stairs, she tried to send calming thoughts into her mind. She didn't succeed.

Maggie stepped into the kitchen. She froze.

Sam bumped into her. "Maggie? What's wrong?"

"That. Look. There. On the table."

"Your washing basket?" Sam moved over to it. "And?"

"I didn't bring my washing in. It was on the line when I left the house earlier."

"Could one of your neighbours have brought it in? You said you do that for others sometimes."

Maggie shook her head. "No one has a key." She moved closer to the basket. "I never fold the clothes that neatly when I take them off the line. And that T-shirt on the top," she gulped, "that isn't my T-shirt."

Chapter 26

Maggie stared at the T-shirt in horror. It was bright green, and it had a huge hedgehog on the front. The hedgehog was looking through a pair of binoculars. A speech bubble next to the creature contained the words 'BOO! I can see you!'

Sam began to take photos of the T-shirt and the washing basket. He said to Maggie, "Don't move. Don't touch anything. I'm going to take photos of everything. I'll send them to DCI Dexter, and demand he gets a team around here straight away to investigate this. No more excuses."

Maggie didn't move from the spot as Sam moved around the house. Her mind went blank as if it had shut down in horror. She couldn't take her eyes off the hedgehog T-shirt.

She wasn't even aware of Sam's return until he put a warm hand on her shoulder. "Maggie, look at me."

She reluctantly tore her attention away from the T-shirt. She gave him a questioning look, her mind unable to think of what to say.

"Maggie, we have to leave right now. The person who came into your house could be watching our every move. I've made a quick sweep of your house, and I can't detect any surveillance bugs, but it was only a quick sweep. Do you understand what I'm saying?"

Maggie nodded, still at a loss for words.

"You have to pack some things. We have to leave now. Right now. Okay? Maggie, do you understand?"

She broke into a smile. "We're leaving. Yes, I understand. I'll get my suitcase ready."

"No, we don't have time. Maggie, someone could be watching us."

"My suitcase is on top of the wardrobe. Would you mind getting it down for me, please? I have got a stepladder, but it's in the shed. And I don't want to go out there and disturb the hedgehogs. They might be sleeping behind the shed. They do that sometimes." She smiled. "The little scamps."

"Maggie!" Sam shouted. He gave her a none too gentle shake. "Maggie! We have to leave now. Your life is in danger. Do you understand?"

Maggie blinked at him a few times. Then her brain woke up. "We have to leave? But I can't just leave! I need things. And clothes! And my bits and pieces!"

"We don't have time for your bits and pieces."

She gave him a grim look. "I need my bits and pieces. I'm not going anywhere without them. I'll be two minutes." She dashed out of the kitchen and rushed upstairs.

Sam yelled, "Don't bring a big bag!"

"I'll bring whatever bag I want," she yelled back.

"Bring your passport!"

Passport? Why would she need that? Oh, probably for official identification. Fair enough.

It was only when she got to her bedroom that Maggie realised she didn't know how long she'd be away from her house. Or where Sam was intending to take her.

"It'll only be a day or two," she reassured herself as confidently as she could. "Just while the police sort everything out. Yes. Just a day or two."

She grabbed a medium-sized bag from the bottom of her wardrobe and began to stuff some clothes into it. She put in a pair of pyjamas and a few changes of underwear. A quick visit to the bathroom to collect her bits and pieces, and then she was done. She had enough to keep her going for at least two days. She wouldn't be away any longer than that.

Sam was pacing about the kitchen when she returned.

"I'm ready," she announced. "Where are we going?"

He put a finger to his lips.

That action made Maggie stiffen. Was someone listening to them? Had he found a recording device somewhere?

She nodded in understanding. In silence, they left Maggie's house. She locked it even though she knew locks wouldn't keep out the evil person who had recently invaded it.

As they drove away, Maggie asked, "Where are we going?"

"I'm not sure yet. Have you got any cash on you?"

"A bit. But I've got my bank card."

Sam shot her a look. "Don't use your card. Not for anything. It can be traced. I'll get cash from my supplies."

"Right." Maggie gave him an uncertain look. She pulled her handbag a bit closer in case he suddenly felt the need to destroy her bank cards. "When will I be able to return home?"

Sam didn't look at her as he drove along. And he didn't answer her.

Maggie didn't ask him again.

Chapter 27

They didn't talk as Sam drove them into Leeds and towards his shop. Maggie had lots of questions, but she didn't ask them as she was too scared to hear the answers. She felt numb but somehow alert too. It was like her mind was protecting her from processing any information, but her body was ready to flee from any danger.

Sam parked the van in a small courtyard behind his shop. He said slowly, "We're going inside now. I need to make some arrangements. I won't be long. You'll have to come with me because I won't be using the van again for a while."

"You don't have to talk to me as if I'm stupid, you know."

"I know you're not stupid, but you are in shock."

"I'm not."

"You are. And you're in denial too."

"I am not. I'll wait here for you."

"Maggie, you have to get out."

"Why?"

"We won't be using the van."

"Why not?"

"We'll be using other forms of transport."

Maggie nodded. "I'll wait here until I know where we're going."

"There's no point waiting in the van. We won't be using it again." Sam's voice rose slightly.

She tutted. "There's no need to shout."

Sam rubbed his forehead but didn't say anything. He opened the driver's door and got out. Then he waited outside Maggie's door until she got out too. He offered to take her bag, but she told him she could manage, thank you very much.

Maggie followed Sam through the back entrance of the shop. She didn't know why she was being so mean to him. He was a lovely man. But her thoughts and words were somehow not her own.

She followed the sound of voices and found Sam talking to Jake in the main part of the shop. Sam was crouching by the floorboard safe. He was taking things out and shoving them into a small, tatty backpack.

Jake gave Maggie a quick nod of hello, and then continued talking to his dad. "How long will you be gone?"

Sam closed the floor safe, straightened up, and said, "I don't know. This is a tricky one. You know how to contact me. I'm not sure how long I'll keep this phone. But you know the protocol." He sighed and put his hand on Jake's shoulder. "Keep safe. We're dealing with a professional killer. Maybe more than one."

Jake patted his dad's hand, and then took it from his shoulder. "Dad, I know what to do. I've done it before. But will she—" He stopped talking and looked away.

Maggie said, "You can say anything in front of me. I don't think I can be shocked again today."

"I doubt that," Jake said. "I was going to ask Dad if you'll be safe. Dad's just told me about your house. If someone's out to get you, they won't stop until they do get you. They probably want you dead."

"Jake!" Sam exploded. "That's enough."

"But she has to know. This is serious. We're used to it, but she isn't. Why don't you take her to the police station? Tell them to lock her in a cell until it's safe."

"They won't do that," Sam replied.

Jake turned to Maggie. "You should commit a crime, and then get locked up. Punch Dad. Slash the van's tyres. Do something illegal."

"I'll do no such thing!" Maggie retorted. "And I don't want to be locked up in the police station either. I'll be safe with your dad. I don't know where he's taking me, but I trust him."

Jake smiled at that. "You can trust him with your life. Actually, you *are* trusting him with your life."

Maggie suddenly felt guilty. And weak. She should be able to take care of herself. She'd been doing it for years. She said to Sam, "Once you've taken me to a safe place, you can leave me. I'm sure you've got plenty to do here."

Sam shook his head. "I'm not leaving you. We're in this together. And that's my choice. Don't even think of arguing with me." He gave her a firm nod to confirm his words. "Jake, you get on with things here. I noticed some CCTV cameras near Maggie's street. See what you can find on them. We should be getting something back about the identity of the man who was murdered, soon. Can you chase that up?"

"Of course."

"I know I shouldn't ask you this, but don't tell your mum about, you know."

Jake smirked. "That you've gone on the run with a woman you only met yesterday? I won't tell her that."

Sam gave him a little push. "I didn't mean that, but yes, don't tell her. If she gives you any info about the murder, pass it on to me." He abruptly pulled his son into an embrace, patted his back, and then released him.

Jake looked stunned. "Dad? What's wrong? What aren't you telling me?"

Sam dismissed Jake's concerns with a wave of his hand. "I've told you everything you need to know. Take good care of yourself. Be safe. Extra safe. I'll see you soon. I love you."

Worry filled Jake's face. He nodded slowly at his dad, and then sat down in front of one of the computers.

Maggie was fully aware of Jake's distress. She had a strong urge to give Jake a hug, but knew it was inappropriate. But maybe she should anyway.

She moved towards Jake, but Sam put his hand up to stop her. He shook his head as if he knew what her intention was. Her shoulders dropped, and she returned his nod.

Sam gave her a tight-lipped smile. He said, "Are you ready?"

"Yes," she said firmly, even though she didn't know where they were going, or how long they'd be away.

She had the strongest feeling that her life was about to change beyond recognition.

Chapter 28

Before they left the shop, Sam did something on his phone. Then he gave Jake a swift nod, and said, "It's all in place. Take care."

"I always do." Jake's smile was grim. "You keep safe too. Both of you."

Maggie was reluctant to leave the relative safety of the shop, but a gentle push from Sam forced her out to the street.

"Now what?" Maggie asked. "Where are we going?"

"I'm not sure yet, but we'll soon know. Let's head to the train station." His smile was confident. Maggie didn't know how he was managing to do that.

As they headed along Briggate and towards the station, a scruffy man holding a can of lager wobbled towards them. He gave them a gummy smile. Maggie deftly stepped to the side, but Sam wasn't quick enough.

"Hey up!" the scruffy man said to Sam. "Spare any money for a drink, pal? I've nearly finished with this one." He waggled the can in Sam's face.

Sam replied politely, "I haven't got any cash on me. Sorry."

The man put a filthy hand on Sam's chest. "You must have something. Come on, pal. Do me a favour." He lifted the can to his lips and drank whatever was left.

Sam patted his pockets. "I really am sorry. I don't have anything."

The man shot Sam a look which was filthier than his coat. This was followed by a loud burp and a couple of swear words. The man thrust the empty can into Sam's chest and then wobbled away.

Sam gave Maggie an apologetic look. "I really don't have any money. I would have given him some if I had. I'll just get rid of this can."

Maggie nodded.

Sam put the can in a recycling bin and returned to her side. He glanced behind him, frowned, and then looked back at her. "I keep getting the feeling we're being followed. It's probably just my suspicious nature."

Maggie looked behind her. "I'm getting that feeling too. Can we hurry?"

Sam nodded, and they increased their speed as they walked on.

But they were soon interrupted by a woman in a bright yellow coat who was holding a clipboard. Maggie had already seen her on the path ahead and had veered off in a different direction. But Sam wasn't as lucky. The woman fixed her bright eyes on Sam and made a beeline for him. Sam tried his best to step out of her way, but he was no match for the determined woman. Maggie reckoned these people with clipboards had special training when it came to identifying weak targets.

Maggie watched Sam as he tried to dodge the woman's questions. To her credit, the woman was extremely persistent. She even managed to give Sam a couple of leaflets for whatever she was selling. Sam kept nodding and smiling, whilst taking sideways steps away from the woman.

It took him a few minutes to extricate himself fully. He went over to Maggie with another apologetic look. "Sorry about that. I don't know why they always go for me. I must have a certain look."

"What was she selling? Holidays? Windows?"

Sam shoved the leaflets in his pocket. "I wasn't listening. Maggie, have you been in touch with your son lately?"

"I sent him a text last night." They carried on walking. "He's got a lot of meetings planned for today. Again. He's so busy these days." She hesitated. "Should I contact him now? Are we going to be away for a while?"

"It's okay. You can contact him. Just don't tell him where you're going."

"I don't know where we're going, so that won't be hard."

They crossed the road which led to the train station.

Sam said, "When we do know where we're going, don't tell him. It's for his own safety."

Maggie's stomach clenched at his words, but she didn't ask him to elaborate. He was probably exaggerating. Oscar wasn't in any danger. Was he?

They stopped in the middle of the train station entrance. Maggie looked at the departure boards. "Do you know where we're going yet?" she asked. Sam didn't answer, so she looked at him to see he was reading the leaflets the clipboard woman had given him. "Is this any time to be looking at them? Aren't we supposed to be fleeing?"

Sam peeled something from the leaflets. He handed one to Maggie. "Here's your train ticket."

Maggie's eyebrows rose. "Where did you get this from?"

"From my contact."

"Your contact? You mean the woman with the clipboard?"

Sam nodded. "Yes. I sent a few messages out before we left my shop." He looked at his ticket. "Looks like we're going to Morecambe. I've never been there before. Have you?"

Maggie couldn't speak. What universe had she entered where people passed secret train tickets to each other on the streets of Leeds?

Sam pointed to the board. "Platform sixteen. Let's get a coffee before we board." He strode towards the barriers as if he were going a day trip.

Maggie silently followed him. Her mind couldn't handle any of this and was starting to shut down again.

Chapter 29

Maggie remained silent as she went after Sam through the barriers. Up the escalators and across the concourse they went. Sam stopped for a coffee at the nearest vendor. Maggie finally spoke, and ordered a mint tea. She needed something to settle her nerves.

Sam whistled happily as they went down the other escalator and onto platform sixteen. He checked his ticket, and said, "We've got a couple of changes on the way. It makes the journey more exciting, don't you think?"

"I don't know what to think. I can't find any words." She took a sip of her mint tea. It was far too hot, and it burnt her tongue. But the sudden pain cleared her head. She whispered, "What will we do when we get to Morecambe? Do you have any contacts there? How many contacts do you have around Leeds? Are some watching us right now? Are they criminals? People you've done work for who are repaying a favour?"

Sam smiled. "I thought you couldn't find any words?" He nodded towards the end of the platform. "The train's here. I'll explain more on the train. One thing I can tell you is that I don't work for criminals. Apart from those who have seen the error of their ways, and reformed."

"That doesn't fill me with confidence."

The train pulled up, and they got on. They took opposite seats across a table and put their drinks down. Maggie gave everyone who boarded the train a long look. Was one of them the killer? That old man in the glasses and a tweed flat cap? That young woman in tatty jeans with a battered backpack? She didn't know who she was searching for but thought it wise to look at everyone anyway.

When the train had pulled out of the station, Sam explained more. "I have a lot of contacts around the country. And some in other countries. In case we need them."

Maggie's eyes narrowed. "Why would we need to leave the country?"

He shrugged in answer. "You never know. I have a network of people who I can trust, and who will provide me with certain things in a hurry. Such as train tickets. I do the same for them if needed. Do you want anything to eat? The food trolley is coming this way."

"I'm not hungry, thanks." Maggie gave him a suspicious look. "That man who bumped into you, the drunk, was he a contact too?"

"He was. Well worked out. That was Kevin. He's a master of disguise. He loves playing a drunk as he gets to swear a lot." Sam leaned on the table and lowered his voice. "He left a wad of money inside that lager can. We've got plenty. Give me your hand." He held his hand out.

Maggie put her hand in his. His other hand went over hers, and she felt him nudging something into her palm. She took her hand back, lowered it beneath the table, and then looked at what Sam had put there.

Her breath caught in her throat. She looked back at Sam with wide eyes. She mouthed, "How much?"

He held four fingers up.

"Four hundred?" Maggie mouthed, her hand curling around the roll of money.

He shook his head.

"Four thousand?"

He nodded.

Maggie's palms suddenly felt sweaty. She had never held that much money before. She pulled her handbag onto her knee and put the money into a zipped pocket inside the bag. She kept her handbag on her knee.

She said quietly, "Why do I need so much money?"

"For accommodation. Food. Anything you might need. We can't use cards. I've got the same amount, and I can get more if needed."

"But we don't need this much, do we? I'll be back home soon. Won't I?"

"Ah, here's the food trolley. Are you sure you don't want anything? This journey will take a while. Why don't you get something anyway? Just in case."

Maggie's eyes stung with unshed tears as worry set in. Would she ever return home?

Sam ordered a ham and cheese sandwich, and two chocolate bars. Maggie ordered the same even though she wasn't that keen on ham. She seemed incapable of making decisions.

Once the food trolley had passed on down the aisle, Sam said, "Don't look so worried. It will be okay. You'll return home at some point. Jake will find out what we need to know. And then everything will get sorted out. Try to eat something. You need to keep your strength up."

Maggie managed to eat one of the chocolate bars. She stared out at the passing scenery and thought about her home. She should be doing her big shop at the supermarket this afternoon. She was low on washing powder and toilet rolls. She had certain things she did at certain times during the week. And they didn't include an impromptu train ride to the seaside with a man she barely knew.

She suddenly stiffened, and looked at her train ticket. It was a one-way ticket. How was she going to get home?

Then she remembered the money in her handbag and relaxed a little. It was okay. She would return home soon. She would make sure of that.

Chapter 30

The killer munched on a sandwich. The ham was far too dry, and there was barely any cheese. Well, that was train food for you.

The killer smiled at the worried expression on Maggie's face. She should be worried. And scared. Things were going to get much worse for her.

The thought almost made the killer laugh. Suddenly, the sandwich didn't taste that bad.

Chapter 31

Maggie and Sam changed trains twice before reaching the seaside town of Morecambe. The sight of the sea lifted Maggie's spirits a little. She had been here years ago with Harry when they'd only been married a few years. They'd had a wonderful time, as people in love do wherever they are.

Sam said, "Shall we have a walk along the seafront? It'll do us good to stretch our legs. Isn't there a statue of Eric Morecambe somewhere? He was one of my favourite comedians. He still is."

"How long are we staying here, Sam?" Maggie couldn't keep the worry from her voice.

"At least for one night." He scanned the seafront. "I think the statue is over that way."

"If we're staying here tonight, shouldn't we find somewhere to sleep?" Her voice rose. "Or are you expecting us to sleep on the beach? Is that what happens in your world?"

"Maggie, calm down. You don't need to shout."

"I do! This might be normal for you. Just taking off to a town, and then strolling around as if you're on holiday. But it's not normal for me. I need to know where I'm sleeping tonight. Is that too much to ask?"

"No, of course not," Sam said in a soothing tone. He pointed to their left. "I spotted a line of bed and breakfast places over there. They've all got vacancies. We could try a hotel, but a lot of them want card details even when you pay in cash. Which we don't want to do."

Maggie looked at where Sam had pointed. "Can we book into a bed and breakfast now? I'd feel better if I knew I had somewhere to sleep. Somewhere to call home for a night."

"Okay. We'll do that now." He smiled at her. "Eric's statue isn't going anywhere. I can look at him later. I might get some fish and chips too. You have to eat fish and chips at the seaside. It's the law."

His words made her smile slightly. She said, "Thanks."

They booked themselves into the first guest house they came to. The landlady was so friendly and welcoming that Maggie almost burst into tears.

But she refrained herself. She had to keep a tight rein on her emotions and act like everything was normal.

Sam insisted on having rooms next to each other, which Maggie didn't object to. She wanted him nearby.

They stopped at their respective doors. Sam said to her, "You can stay in your room for the rest of the day if that's what you want. We can meet in the morning."

She shook her head. "I don't want to be alone. Can you give me fifteen minutes or so? To freshen up. Is it okay if I phone my son?"

"Of course. You don't need my permission for that. Or for anything. I'll meet you downstairs in a bit." He smiled before going into his room.

Maggie let herself into her room. It was cheerful and clean. There were lots of little touches around the room which gave it a welcoming feel. Things like scented candles, a shelf full of books, and a bowl of fresh fruit. She didn't unpack because she didn't have much to unpack. And also, she wasn't intending to stay here for long. She'd be returning home soon.

She sat on the bed and phoned Oscar.

"Mum! Hi! I was beginning to worry about you. Are you okay?"

"I'm fine, love. How are you? How did your meetings go?"

"Really well. We've got some exciting projects lined up. Mum, are you okay? You sound tired."

"I am a bit. Tell me more about your projects."

Oscar did so. His enthusiastic voice made Maggie smile. She loved that he was so happy in his job. When Harry had died, she wasn't sure either one of them would feel such joy again. But Oscar had. And she was getting better at not feeling sad all the time.

Oscar finished talking about his job. "Mum, are you sure you're okay? You haven't spoken about the neighbours, and what they're up to. You've usually got something to tell me."

"Not today. I've been too busy with other things to look at what the neighbours are doing."

"What kind of things? What have you been up to? Anything exciting?"

She hesitated. She was so tempted to tell him. But then Sam's warning words about Oscar's safety came to her mind. "Oh, nothing that exciting. What are your plans for tomorrow?"

"Never mind me. Mum, why don't you go to Brighton? The sea air would do you good."

Maggie glanced out of the window at the sea view. "I don't need to go to Brighton. Don't worry about me."

Oscar carried on. "Don't be mad, but I spoke to Carmella about you earlier today."

"You did? Why?"

"Because you need a holiday. Time away from the house. I thought if I spoke to Carmella, then she would phone you and tell you to go." His voice softened. "She asked about my work. She's always interested in my work. She's so kind. So thoughtful. A lovely woman."

Maggie shook her head at Oscar's comments. "What did Carmella say about me? Does she agree with you?"

There was an offended tone in his voice. "She said I should mind my own business, and let you make your own decisions."

Maggie laughed. "She's right about that. I'll let you go now. You must have plenty to do."

"I don't have to rush off. Did Carmella give you the keys to that house in Brighton? Doesn't it belong to a friend of hers? Did she say whether the friend was male or female?"

"She said it was a female friend. And yes, I do still have the keys and the address in my handbag just in case I feel the need to go there."

"I hope you do go."

There was a soft knock at Maggie's door. She said to Oscar, "I'll say goodbye now. Love you loads. I'll speak to you tomorrow." She ended the call before Oscar got the chance to say anything else.

She opened the door to Sam's stern-looking face. He said quietly, "I have some news. But I can't tell you it here."

Chapter 32

Maggie grabbed her handbag before leaving the room. They headed for the beach, and walked along the seafront. When they were far enough away from other people, Sam indicated for them to sit on a bench.

Maggie sat down and looked out to sea. A seagull screeched overhead. She waited for Sam to speak.

He finally did. "Jake's found out the identity of the man who was murdered."

Maggie's head turned to look at him so quickly that she almost pulled a muscle. "He has? That's great news." She grinned widely at Sam. "Isn't it?"

"It is. Sort of."

Maggie's grin died. "What do you mean?"

"His name was William Phelps."

"Oh." Maggie's head tipped to the side. "He didn't look like a William. I thought he looked more like a Fergus or Bertram."

Sam gave her a curious look, shook his head, and said, "Anyway. It took a while for Jake to find out his name because, and this is the bad news, William Phelps was in a witness protection scheme. It's actually called the UK Protected Persons Service."

Maggie's nose wrinkled. "Is that a real thing? Witness protection, or that other thing you called it."

"Of course it is. Why wouldn't it be?"

"I thought it was just something that happened in movies."

"Well, it is a real thing. And our Mr Phelps was in it. Which means it's going to be difficult to find out anything about his past." Sam turned in his seat to look at Maggie better. "From your intensive knowledge of crime movies, what do you know about witness protection schemes?"

"I don't care for the sarcastic tone in your voice, Mr Ward. But I assume a person in that scheme has a new identity, and they're placed in a new town."

Sam nodded. "Those are the basics. And it's usually handled by the local police force."

"Does that mean the police in Leeds will know about William Phelps and his history? They will, won't they? If they don't know, you can tell them now.

They can find out who he really was, and then investigate his past, and who wanted to kill him."

Sam sighed. "I wish it were that simple. Don't forget your recording device was stolen from the police station. I don't want to give the police such sensitive information about your neighbour if there's a chance that information could be discovered by the wrong person. Also, William Phelps could have family who are still in the scheme."

"Oh. Right. So, what's going to happen next?"

He gave her one of his confident smiles. "I'm going to call in my favours, use my contacts, and all my resources. We'll find out about Mr Phelps and his real identity. Then we'll be able to investigate his past."

Maggie's heart sank. "I can't ask you to do that. I don't want you using all your favours up on me."

"You haven't asked me to do it. I'm offering to do it." He sniffed the air. "I can smell chips. Are you hungry? I fancy some fish and chips. What about you?"

Maggie said, "I haven't eaten that sandwich from the train yet. Are you always hungry?"

"Yep." He stood up. "Come on. There's a fish and chip shop over there. I'll buy you a bag of chips if you're lucky." He held his hand out to her.

Maggie took it as she stood up. Why were his hands always so warm? She quickly took her hand back. "I might manage a bag of chips. They do smell nice. Sam, what's going to happen next? When you find out about William Phelps and his past?"

"One step at a time." They set off towards the shop. "Let me take your mind off it by telling you about some of my earlier cases. I was such an innocent man until I started working in surveillance. Would you like to hear about my earlier cases?"

"I wouldn't mind."

"I won't tell you the more sordid ones."

"I could manage sordid," Maggie replied with a small smile. "I'm not as delicate as I look."

They bought some food and then strolled along the beach as the sky turned darker. Maggie listened with interest to Sam's stories, but she didn't miss how he kept looking over his shoulder as if expecting to see someone there.

Once they'd finished eating, Sam said, "We should head back to the bed and breakfast. Do you think you'll be able to sleep?"

"I already know I won't. My head is full of a thousand worries."

Sam nodded in understanding. "In that case, we can sit in the lounge area at the bed and breakfast for a while. We can play cards and games until you're utterly exhausted. I can tell you some more stories too. Those are bound to make you fall asleep."

"I don't want to keep you up all night."

"I'm not at all tired," he replied brightly. "I'm as fresh as a daisy. As lively as a spring chicken. As...energetic as someone with lots of energy."

From the darkening shadows under his eyes, Maggie knew he was lying. But she appreciated his kindness. Even though she was trying to deny her feelings, she was becoming more fond of him with every passing minute.

Was that such a bad thing?

Chapter 33

Maggie slept surprisingly well that night. Possibly due to the large glass of whisky she'd had before bed. She didn't even like whisky that much, but the landlady had insisted on making them both a nightcap as they'd played a board game in the lounge. The strength of the nightcap had seared Maggie's throat, but the warmth in her stomach had soon made her forget about that.

The landlady had poured herself a glass of whisky too, and then sat between Maggie and Sam, and talked incessantly about her adventurous life as a landlady. The sound of her lilting voice was like a lullaby to Maggie. By the time her head hit the pillow, Maggie was already falling asleep.

Maggie got out of bed and took a quick shower using the supplied toiletries. They weren't her usual brand, but they were pleasant enough.

After sending a message to Oscar wishing him a lovely day at work, Maggie left her room and knocked on Sam's door. She yelped when he opened it.

"Crikey! You look rough," she announced. "Haven't you slept?"

He ran a hand over his bristly chin. "I slept a bit, but I was up most of the night. I've been talking to Jake a lot. I wanted to know how he was getting on with things."

"Has he been up most of the night too?"

"He's used to it. He likes working through the night. I think he's half-vampire." Sam tried to stifle a yawn, but failed.

Maggie said, "I'm sorry to be insensitive considering you've been up most of the night, but do you know when I can go home?"

"It'll be a few more days yet. At least. Jake is making some headway. I'll keep checking on him." He yawned again.

"Okay. Sam, thanks for what you're doing for me. Say thanks to Jake too when you next speak to him."

"I will do."

"If we're going to be here a few more days, I could do with some more clothes. I'll pop out to the shops and have a look. You stay here. I won't be long."

"No."

"No? To what?" Maggie lifted her chin.

"No to you going on your own. I'll come with you."

"But you look exhausted. You need more sleep."

"I'm fine. Come in a minute. I'll get my things, and have a quick wash." He opened the door wider and walked away.

Maggie stepped into the room. The carefully placed cushions were still in place on the bed which indicated it hadn't been slept in. Had Sam managed any sleep?

Sam came out of the bathroom looking a tad fresher. He grabbed his jacket, and said, "Let's go. What clothes do you need?"

Maggie needed underwear, but she wasn't going to tell him that. "Just a couple of tops. Maybe some trousers. Perhaps a skirt or two. Some comfy shoes. A waterproof jacket because I've only got this one which I'm wearing. It's useless in the rain. And some shampoo, conditioner, body wash, body moisturiser. I forgot to bring some, in the rush."

Sam stared at her. His mouth slowly dropped open.

"I'm okay for make-up," Maggie concluded. "I'll have a think on the way for anything else I might need. Are you ready to go?"

Sam's mouth closed. He gave her a nod, and said, "Let's not be too long."

"We won't. We'll be back before you know it."

Sam let out a groan. "Famous last words."

Chapter 34

Before they left the bed and breakfast, Sam spoke to the landlady and asked for another night's accommodation. The landlady beamed at them and wrote their names in the register. Maggie had a quick word with the landlady about the shops in Morecambe. Maggie's heart sank as she listened to her detailed reply. Maggie knew this was no time to be picky about which shops to visit, but she couldn't help it.

Sam noticed her disappointment as they left the building. "What's wrong?" he asked.

"I wanted to go to a certain shop, but they don't have one here. The nearest one is in Lancaster, which isn't that far away. We'd have to get the bus there."

"Then that's what we'll do. Did our friendly landlady tell you which bus to get?"

"She did." Maggie pointed to a bus stop a short distance away. "They're every ten minutes."

"Right. We'll get the bus, then."

"Are you sure? I could have a look at the shops here instead."

"It's no problem." Sam strode towards the bus stop whilst doing his peculiar surveillance walk.

Maggie caught up with him. "If it's no problem, then why do you keeping looking left, right, and over your shoulder all the time? Are we being followed?"

"Not that I can see." He gave her a shrug. "It's just how I walk when I'm out. Jake does it too. It's wise to be aware of your surroundings, and your escape routes."

Maggie shook her head. "We're living in different worlds."

"Not at the moment, we aren't." Sam stuck his hand out as a bus appeared. They got on. He paid in cash for the fares. They sat upstairs on the back seat.

Maggie asked him, "How far has Jake got with his enquiries? I saw you on the phone when I was talking to the landlady. I assumed it was Jake."

"Jake's making good progress," was Sam's enigmatic reply. He suddenly sat up straighter. "Breakfast! We haven't had breakfast. We can't go shopping on an empty stomach."

96

Maggie fished a chocolate bar from her bag and gave it to him. "Will this do?"

"For now. Thanks." He ripped the wrapper open and tore into the bar like a ravenous lion.

They soon arrived in Lancaster, and Maggie headed towards her favourite shop.

Sam said, "Marks and Spencer's? That's why we came here?"

Maggie nodded. "They have everything I need in here. They never let me down."

She walked into the shop. Her heart lifted. It was so wonderfully familiar. The lighting. The rows of carefully hung clothes with plenty of space between rails. Everything organised into sensible areas. The quiet murmurings of customers. No loud music. No pushy salespeople. Everything was calm and organised.

Maggie caught Sam smiling at her. "What?" she asked.

"You look so happy. It's just a shop."

Maggie let out a mock gasp of outrage. "Just a shop? It's not just a shop. This is heaven. It's peace and quiet. Look at the customers. No one's shoving each other. No one is raising their voice." She put her hand on her chest. "I feel like I've come home. Like everything is safe again. I don't have to think about murdered neighbours here. Not for a while."

Sam nodded. "Fair enough. Do they have a café here?"

"They will have." Maggie glanced towards the display board, and then told Sam where the café was. "I'll meet you there in thirty minutes or so."

"No."

"No what? I thought you were hungry."

"I'm starving, but I'm not leaving you alone. I'll come with you."

"No," Maggie said firmly. "I'll be fine. Nothing's going to happen to me in the middle of Marks and Spencer's."

"You don't know that. I'm coming with you." He gave her such an intense look that Maggie took a step back.

Knowing she was beaten, she said, "Okay. But don't rush me."

"I won't." His stomach rumbled. "But don't be long."

Maggie gave him a withering look and then walked towards the clothes area. She knew what she was looking for. She picked similar items to things she already had at home. She didn't even need to try them on. Two blouses, two pairs of trousers, a cardigan, and a set of comfy pyjamas. She picked the value items, not the more expensive ones. She didn't bother with the skirts or dresses because she'd have to buy tights and shoes to go with them. And she didn't want to take too long because Sam kept giving her impatient looks for some reason.

She walked towards the waterproof jackets. Sam trailed after her, with a rumbling coming from his stomach area now and again. She said to him, "Should I bother with a waterproof jacket? Or should I make do with my umbrella and this jacket I'm wearing? It doesn't look like it's going to rain soon. And the weatherman didn't mention rain for this week. What do you think?"

With barely controlled patience, he muttered, "I don't care. Have you nearly finished? I need food."

"I'll make do with my umbrella," she said with a nod. "Go to the café. I'm almost done."

"Almost done? What else do you need? You've got nearly the whole shop in your arms."

Maggie stared at him. "There is no need to raise your voice at me. And I haven't got half the shop in my arms."

Sam let out a heavy sigh. "Sorry. I'm bad-tempered because I'm hungry."

"I know. So go to the café. I won't be long. I'll be over there." She nodded her head quickly in the direction of the underwear department.

"No."

"Let's not start this again," Maggie said. "I need some underwear, and I don't want you looking over my shoulder while I look for some."

Sam blinked. "I won't look over your shoulder, but I am coming with you. You won't be long, will you? It doesn't take long to buy underwear."

She shook her head at him. Little did he know. She resigned herself to the fact he was coming with her and walked over to the underwear.

She'd only been looking at packs of knickers for one minute, when Sam said in her ear, "Get that pack. You get five in that one." He pointed at something on the rack.

Maggie tutted. "Thongs? I don't wear thongs. Do I look like I wear thongs?"

Sam muttered, "I don't know." He took a few steps away from her, picked a multipack up and thrust it at her. "These will do."

Maggie looked in horror at the multipack. "Maternity knickers! Do I look pregnant? Do I?" She sucked her stomach in. "Do you think I look pregnant? Answer me, Sam."

Sam held his hands up in defence. "I didn't know they were maternity knickers. And no, I don't think you look pregnant. You wouldn't be pregnant anyway, not at your age, would you?"

Maggie threw the multi-pack at his head. He ducked, and the packet flew past him and landed in front of a startled shop assistant.

Sam said, "Sorry, I didn't mean—"

"You think I'm fat and old!" Maggie glowered at him. There was a quiet, civilised voice in her head telling her to calm down, and to remind her she was in the middle of Marks and Spencer's. But she was too angry to listen to that voice. "Fat and old! That's what you think of me, isn't it? You're only helping me because you feel sorry for me!"

"That's not true at all. Maggie, calm down. Stop shouting."

"Don't you tell me what to do! I saw my neighbour getting murdered! The police think I'm a liar! I've got hedgehogs all over my living room! I've had to flee from my house without even leaving money for the window cleaner with a neighbour! I'm trying my best to deal with this nightmare without falling to pieces. And all I wanted to do was come here and buy some comfy underwear. But no, you had to come with me, and then you called me fat and old! Is that fair, Sam? Is it? IS IT?"

A concerned shop assistant came scuttling over. She put her arm around Maggie's shoulders, and gave Sam a disgusted look. She said to him curtly, "Go and sit over there with the other husbands."

"But I'm not—" Sam tried to argue.

"Now, sir. Go now." The shop assistant's tone was beyond stern. "I will look after your wife."

Sam tried again. "But she's not—"

"Now." The shop assistant wasn't one for arguments.

Sam's head dropped in defeat. He trudged over to a line of chairs outside the changing rooms. Two of the seats were occupied by men wearing expressions of tired resignation. They gave Sam understanding smiles as he sat next to them. One of them gave Sam his newspaper.

Embarrassed heat ran through Maggie. She said to the shop assistant, "I'm so sorry. I don't know what came over me."

"That's okay. No need to explain. I'm married too. Now then, let's get you sorted out. What are you looking for today?"

Maggie turned her back on Sam and spoke to the shop assistant about her needs. The assistant nodded, then like the professional she was, she quickly gathered items for Maggie in the perfect style, size and colours. Maggie hadn't even needed to tell the lovely woman what size she was.

Once her purchases were complete, Maggie collected Sam from his chair.

She said to him, "I'm so very sorry. I never get that angry. I don't know what happened to me."

Sam surprised her by taking her into his arms. "It's okay. I deserved it. I'm the one who was in the wrong." He kissed the top of her head, and then released her. He smiled. "You look even more beautiful when you're angry. All bright-eyed and full of energy. Can we go to the café now, please?"

She nodded. He'd called her beautiful. No one had called her that since Harry had died. She didn't know how she felt about Sam's comment, so she buried it away and didn't think about it at all.

Chapter 35

Maggie felt much better as they returned to the bed and breakfast two hours later. Sam had a full stomach, and she had fresh underwear. Sam had insisted on buying toiletries for her, and he'd paid for the luxury versions instead of the basic ones which Maggie normally bought. She tried to argue about needing to save money, but he had told her he could get more money if needed.

As they headed towards their rooms, Sam said to her, "I'll catch up with Jake and see how far he's got. Hopefully, he should have some news for us. I'll have a quick shower first. I need to wake myself up."

"Okay. I'll phone Oscar. See you in a bit."

"Okay."

"Right."

They looked at each other with silly smiles on their faces for a few seconds. Then Maggie went into her room.

Everything was going to be okay, she told herself. Sam was taking care of things. He would soon know who the mysterious William Phelps was, and who he'd upset enough to warrant his early demise. And then the police would find the killer, and Maggie would go home.

She smiled. What a story she would have to tell Oscar and Carmella when all this was over!

She emptied her shopping bags onto the bed. She should hang them up. Maybe they could stay here for a while until the killer was caught. That would be nice. They could get to know each other a bit better. Maybe? Hope fluttered in her heart. Was she even considering getting involved with another man?

Maybe.

Maggie took the pyjamas over to the set of drawers under the window. She had this same pair of pyjamas in blue at home. They were very comfy.

She opened the drawer.

She froze.

There was a T-shirt in the drawer. It had a picture of a hedgehog on it. The speech bubble coming from its mouth read, 'Boo! I can see you!'

Maggie pushed the drawer shut. "No! No!"

She opened the drawer beneath that one.

The same T-shirt and message faced her.

Her legs began to shake.

The killer had been in here.

Maggie's hands trembled, and she dropped the pyjamas.

She moved over to the wardrobe and opened the doors. There was a line of hedgehog T-shirts on the hangers. The same message of 'Boo! I can see you' was on every one.

Maggie felt sick. She stumbled into the bathroom. What she saw there caused her knees to buckle. She slowly slithered to the carpet, her back against the tiled wall.

Bright green and red towels hung from the shower cubicle, sink and window. Each had a cheerful hedgehog on it. The message was different this time on the T-shirts:

'So sorry, Maggie, but you have to die. Sorry.'

Maggie forced herself to her feet.

Sam!

She had to tell him about this.

She pushed herself away from the wall and rushed out of her room as quickly as her shaking legs would allow.

She knocked on his door. "Sam! Open up! Sam!"

There was no answer.

She tried the door. It was unlocked. She opened it, went inside and closed the door behind her. "Sam? It's me, Maggie. Sam!"

She heard the sound of a shower going. As scared as she was, she wasn't going to burst into the bathroom if he was having a shower.

She went over to the bed and sat down. How did the killer know she was here? Had they been following her from Leeds? Watching her every move? Had they been watching her meltdown in Marks and Spencer's?

Sam's phone beeped at her side. Maggie nearly jumped out of her skin.

"Sam! Your phone's beeping."

Was it Jake who was sending Sam a message? She should talk to Jake. Tell him about the latest hedgehog development.

She picked Sam's phone up. There was a message on it. Something about an update on security surveillance in Lilac Lane. She frowned at the message, and read it again. Her blood ran cold. She clicked on the message. It took her to a screen which had various screens to look at.

The screens showed rooms.

The rooms were in her house.

Maggie's heart began to race.

Security devices had been placed in her house, in all her rooms.

She clicked on another icon and was shown different screens.

Cameras had been placed outside in her gardens.

The horrific realisation dawned slowly on Maggie.

Sam's phone was linked to the cameras. He must have put the recording devices there.

He'd been watching her house. For how long?

This could only mean one thing.

Sam was the killer.

Maggie stiffened as the noise of the shower ceased.

Sam called out, "Maggie? Are you out there? Hang on, I'm on my way out."

Chapter 36

Somehow, Maggie kept her voice steady as she replied, "Don't rush! I'm not staying. Just wanted to let you know I'm going to have a chat with the landlady. I'll ask her if there's anywhere nice to go for dinner. I shouldn't be too long."

She heard Sam laugh, and then he said, "You'll be ages once she gets talking. If you're not back in ten minutes, I'll come and rescue you."

Maggie was at the door by now. "Okay! See you later."

She dashed out of Sam's room and into hers. Her heart was thumping in her ears.

Sam was the killer.

And she'd been in his company for days.

And she was in a bed and breakfast in Morecambe, and no one knew she was here.

Except Sam the killer.

She had to get out of here right now.

She looked at the shopping she'd just bought, and the large bag she'd brought from home. She couldn't take them. She didn't want Sam to know she'd discovered who he was, and that she'd made a break for it.

Maggie grabbed her handbag and jacket, and left her room. She had a large amount of money to keep her going. She was halfway down the stairs when a thought came to her. She spun around, returned to her room, and put her phone on the bedside table. Now, it looked like she'd only left the room for a while. And Sam had probably bugged her phone anyway.

Thoughts of despair, betrayal and fear fought to gain control of her mind. But she didn't have time for any of them. She needed to think clearly.

As she raced down the stairs, she hoped the landlady wasn't hanging around. She didn't want to get into a discussion about where she was going. Thankfully, the chatty landlady was talking animatedly to a couple in the breakfast room and had her back to Maggie.

Maggie slipped out of the door and was soon rushing along the street.

What was she supposed to do now? Where could she go?

She didn't know. But she had to get as far away from Sam as she could.

A bus went by and stopped at the bus stop a short distance away. Maggie broke into a sprint and raced towards it. It looked like she wasn't going to make it, but a young man was having trouble getting the bus ticket app on his phone to open, which resulted in the bus being held up long enough for Maggie to throw herself on it.

"Where to?" the bus driver asked her.

That was a good question.

"Are you going to the train station?" It was all Maggie could think of.

"I am. Do you want a return ticket?"

"No. Thank you." Maggie paid in cash, and then went upstairs and sat at the back of the bus. It was the same position she'd been in yesterday with Sam. No wonder he kept looking over his shoulder all the time. He was probably looking for the police.

As the bus set off, Maggie's thoughts came crashing down.

Who was Sam Ward, and what work did he really do? He knew a lot about surveillance, so he must work in that field. But who did he do work for? Criminals? Maybe they paid more than non-criminals on account of all the money they made from their illegal work.

Maggie nodded to herself. Yes, that made sense.

And all those contacts he claimed to have around the country? They were no doubt part of his criminal circle of friends. They probably had their own Facebook equivalent on the dark web or something. It was called the dark web, wasn't it?

She nodded again to herself, then stiffened. Was the bus driver part of Sam's network of criminals? Was that old lady in the tartan coat at the front of the bus part of it too?

Sweat broke out on Maggie's forehead. She couldn't trust anyone.

More thoughts dropped into her brain like unwanted guests.

How had Sam managed to put those hedgehog T-shirts and towels in her room while they were out? Oh. Of course. It would have been one of his contacts. He did say they were everywhere.

Did the police know about his illegal activities? Is that really why DCI Dexter was so cold towards him? And what about his ex-wife, Ingrid? Did she know about Sam too? Is that why they really divorced? Maggie recalled all the times Sam had told her the police couldn't help. Had he been lying about that?

The main question was, why had Sam brought her to Morecambe? Obviously, he didn't want her as a witness to his crime, so...

Maggie's eyes stung as the truth hit her. Sam wanted to kill her. She didn't want to die. Not for another thirty or forty years. She had so much to do.

Not that she was doing much with her life at the moment. But she would do someday. She would go travelling. She would make new friends. She would do all the things Oscar kept telling her to do. Someday. And she'd go to all the places in the UK Carmella went to on those spiritual festivals of hers. She always made them sound such fun.

Carmella! Brighton! Of course. Maggie could go there. She checked her handbag for the key and address. They were still there. She had half expected Sam to have taken them out.

It would take hours to get to Brighton, but once she was there, she'd contact the police and let them know everything.

Maggie relaxed a bit. She had a plan. All she had to do now was get to Brighton without any of Sam's contacts seeing her. Or without Sam finding her.

Had he worked out yet that she'd left?

Was he already coming after her?

The bus pulled up next to the train station.

Maggie's mouth set in a determined line as she stood up, She couldn't let fearful thoughts get in her way. She had to do her best to stay alive.

Chapter 37

The killer watched Maggie for a while. The petrified look on Maggie's face had warmed the killer's heart. Serves her right. She should have kept her nose out of things which didn't concern her.

The killer had something important to do next. Something which would rock Maggie's world, and not in a good way.

Chapter 38

Maggie arrived at her destination six hours and two train changes later. She was exhausted, hungry and grubby. She felt like she needed to shower for two hours. Even though she'd been sitting for most of the journey, the horror of the predicament she was in kept playing over and over in her mind. And it had been hard work viewing everyone she saw as a potential contact of Sam's. Even those who looked harmless were given a narrow-eyed look by Maggie.

She'd left her appetite in Morecambe, but knew she had to eat something soon. She knew there was a little café not far from the station. She hoped it was still open at this late hour.

Maggie walked out of the train station, and into the familiar town of Whitby where she'd been many times with her family.

At the last minute, she'd decided against Brighton in case Sam had been listening to her calls. Oscar had mentioned her going to Brighton many times, and he'd also mentioned Carmella's name. It wouldn't take that much sneaky spying work to find Carmella's contact in Brighton, and where she lived.

Anyway, she felt safer in Whitby. It had nothing but good memories for her. And she knew her way around, which helped immensely when Maggie looked for a bed and breakfast a few minutes later.

She found a lovely one a few streets away from the harbour. It was at a good price too. She booked herself in using Sam's dirty money and then headed down to the seafront. She needed to eat something before she going to her room and planning her next move.

Maggie found a little café which was still open and went inside. She scanned the menu and decided she'd be able to eat a toasted cheese sandwich. After giving her order, she chose a table at the back of the café and sat down.

She'd done nothing but think about Sam and the murder for the last six hours, and she couldn't bear to think about that anymore. She let her mind wander, and it landed on her lovely husband. What would Harry have made of this? He would have punched Sam, to begin with. Then he would have told Maggie she could deal with this. Didn't she cope with his death? Didn't she keep going for Oscar's sake? Didn't she take all those jobs to fit in with Oscar's school hours?

Yes, she had. It had been hard at times to keep going, and to not feel sorry for herself. But she'd done it.

Admittedly, she had become stuck in her ways in recent years, but she could do something about that. Get herself out of her comfort zone more.

She smiled to herself. She was well and truly out of her comfort zone now.

The woman behind the counter came over to Maggie and placed the toasted sandwich and tea down. She also placed a big slice of chocolate cake on the table. She gave Maggie a kind smile, and said, "The cake is on the house. You look as if you need it, love."

That thoughtful gesture almost brought Maggie to tears. She said thickly, "Thank you. That's so kind."

The woman patted Maggie's shoulder gently. "Think nothing of it." She gave Maggie a studious look. "Excuse my nosiness, but are you okay?"

"Not really, but I will be." Maggie gave her the best smile she could manage. "Can you tell me where the nearest police station is, please?"

The woman gave her the directions, and said, "Man trouble, is it?"

"Sort of. Will the station be open now?"

"It will, love. They're a lovely bunch too. Helped me out many a time when I've had trouble in here. It's usually the drunks who turn up here. The customers I mean, not the police officers." The woman looked towards the door, and then back at Maggie, "I'm shutting up in a bit. I can go with you to the station, if you like?"

Maggie's suspicions rose. "No, thank you. Actually, I'm not sure if I need to go now. I might phone them instead. Thanks so much for the cake."

"You are more than welcome. You take care, love." The woman walked back over to the counter.

Maggie hated herself for being so suspicious, but she couldn't help it. She ate as quickly as she could even though she knew she was lining up a case of indigestion for herself, and then with a wave at the woman, left the café.

She adopted Sam's quirk of looking left, right, and over her shoulder as she walked towards her room for the night. She'd phone the police from the bed and breakfast. She'd noticed a payphone near the reception desk which took cash. Maybe the police could put her in a witness protection scheme, or whatever Sam said it was called now. Just until Sam was behind bars.

Oh! She had her passport with her. She could leave the country. If she needed to.

Maggie was so lost in all the plans she was making that she didn't notice the person following her through the streets of Whitby.

Until it was too late.

Chapter 39

"Maggie." Someone put a hand on her shoulder.

Maggie spun around.

It was Sam!

"Get off me!" Maggie whacked him around the head with her handbag. Sam cried out in agony and dropped to the ground.

Maggie set off running. How had he found her?

"Maggie! Wait!" he called after her.

No chance, you sneaky, devious, lying, poor excuse of a man.

Maggie ran along the street and turned to her left. She knew these streets. There was a little alleyway just ahead which would take her back to the seafront, and hopefully, towards help.

She turned the next corner, and almost collided into a group of people dressed as vampires. The sight of their ghastly faces made her scream.

One of the vampires laughed, showing sharp teeth. He held his hands out towards her, and said dramatically, "I'm going to bite your neck."

He received a sharp push from his fellow vampire. "Ned! You idiot. Leave her alone." The kind vampire addressed Maggie. "Sorry for my idiot friend. Are you okay? You look scared to death."

Maggie didn't answer. In her confused state, she turned around and headed along another street.

What were vampires doing in Whitby at this time of the year? She knew there was a festival later in the year, but it was months away, wasn't it? Stupid vampires getting in her way.

"Maggie! Wait! It's me, Sam!"

He was running towards her. She saw the pretend look of concern on his face. He was a good actor. He'd certainly fooled her.

Maggie turned into another street and ran on. Her lungs felt like they were going to burst. Her legs were like jelly as she forced them on. Her whole body was going into shock at the amount of unaccustomed exercise she was doing.

All too late, Maggie realised her mistake. She was heading towards the one hundred and ninety-nine steps which led to St Mary's Church and Whitby Abbey.

She had no choice. She had to run up them. Maggie normally struggled walking up them at a leisurely pace. And now, here she was, running up them! Or attempting to. Pure adrenaline and fear kept her going.

For a while.

Her body threw in the towel halfway up the steps. She collapsed onto one of the wider steps, which ironically, had been built to allow coffins to rest on their way to the church.

Maggie gasped for air. She willed her legs to stand up, but they were having none of it. She attempted to lift her hands. Maybe she could push Sam down the steps when he came nearer. But both hands refused to co-operate and rested limply at her sides. She was breathing so heavily that she considered huffing and puffing like the big bad wolf, and blowing him down the steps.

"Maggie?" Sam came closer up the steps.

"Help," Maggie attempted to call out to anyone who was walking past. Her voice was more of a wheeze.

A shadow loomed over her. Sam's face was full of that fake concern as he knelt at her side.

She attempted to bat him away, but it was like hitting a wall. Sam didn't even register her touching him.

"Don't kill me. Please." Maggie blinked away tears. "I don't want to die. Not on Whitby steps. Not anywhere, really."

Sam frowned. "Kill you? I'm not going to kill you."

Maggie let out a groan. "Are you going to torture me? Please, don't do that. I'm not good with pain. I don't even like having my blood taken."

"I'm not going to torture you. Come on; get up." Sam reached out to take her hands. Maggie flinched. A determined look came into Sam's eyes, and he quickly pulled her to her feet.

Her useless legs were too weak to support her, and to her shame, she felt herself resting against Sam. She mumbled into his chest, "Don't kill me. I won't tell anyone you murdered my neighbour. Promise."

Sam put his finger under her chin and tilted it so that Maggie was looking at him. He said, "What are you going on about?"

She pushed his finger away and stood up straighter. Her legs were getting a bit of strength back. "I saw your phone in your room. You've got cameras in my house."

"I know. I put them there."

His honesty made her take a step back. She'd forgotten where she was. She'd taken a step back into nothing. She wobbled on one leg, and like a cartoon character, waved her arms around like helicopter blades as she tried to get her balance.

Sam swiftly put his arms around her and pulled her close. His face turned white. He gulped. "Maggie. Be careful. You nearly fell."

She pulled herself free. "I would have saved you a job if I had fallen. Then you wouldn't have to kill me. Get away from me, you murderer!"

"I'm not a murderer. I swear. I did put those cameras in your house. It was on the day we left, while you were packing. I wanted to see if the murderer came back to your house. But all I've seen so far are those hedgehogs moving around the garden. Look at me. I'm telling you the truth."

Maggie folded her arms. She was not going to look into his brown eyes. "Why did you drag me to Morecambe, eh? It was to get me away from my family and friends, wasn't it?"

"No. I wanted to keep you safe. I gave you a secure phone so you could contact your son." He reached into his pocket and pulled a phone out. "You left this behind in your haste to get away from me."

She folded her arms more tightly. "I don't want your phone."

"Okay." He put the phone back in his pocket.

Maggie's arms dropped. "Just a minute. How did you know I was here in Whitby?"

Sam looked sheepish. "I put a tracker in the bottom of your handbag."

Maggie's eyes went wide. "Why? Oh! I know why! You wanted to know where I am every minute of the day. Am I right?"

"Yes."

"I thought so. And you want to know where I am so you can kill me when the time is right. Is that correct?"

"No. I wish you'd stop saying that."

"Then why did you put a tracker on me?"

"Because I care about you. That's why. You've got yourself involved in a murder, and it seems I'm the only one who can help you. And I want to help you. I was worried the real killer would get to you, so that's why I put the tracker there." His voice cracked a little. "I didn't want anything bad to happen to you."

"Oh."

"Yes, oh. Maggie, if I were the killer, I would have let you fall down the steps just now. If I wanted to murder you, I have had many opportunities to do so." He sighed. "I can see you don't trust me. Look, there's a bench at the top of the steps. Let's sit down, and I'll explain everything."

"I don't want to."

"There are lots of people near the church and Abbey. You can call out for help at any time. I'll even stand a short distance away from you, if that makes you feel safer."

Maggie relented. "Okay. But you go up the steps first. I don't want you behind me, ready to give me a push."

Sam gave her a small smile. "Okay. Would you take your phone, please? I haven't put a tracker on it. Honest."

Maggie reluctantly took the phone. She wasn't used to being without one, but she could always throw this one in a bin when Sam wasn't looking, and then buy a new one.

Sam set off up the steps. "I saw those hedgehog things in your room at the bed and breakfast. I thought the killer had taken you away, until I checked the device I'd put in your handbag. Even then, I wasn't sure until I saw you on your own."

Maggie frowned at his back as she followed him up the steps. Annoyingly, he was making a lot of sense. But she still didn't trust him.

Sam reached the top and headed towards a bench. Maggie followed him, relieved to see a handful of tourists milling around.

Sam stopped about a foot away from the bench and held his hand out towards it.

Maggie sat on the bench, and said primly, "You stay right there. Come any closer, and I'll scream."

He gave her a nod of agreement. "I will, but I've got an update from Jake which you should know. He's found out—" He abruptly stopped talking, frowned, and then suddenly threw himself at Maggie.

Maggie screamed as Sam landed on her.

A gunshot pierced the air.

The sound of it filled Maggie's ears, and she was stunned into silence.

Something warm was seeping into her chest.

Confused, Maggie looked down. Sam was slumped against her chest. It was his blood which was seeping into her.

Maggie screamed and screamed.

Chapter 40

People came dashing over to help her. There were startled gasps, cries of shock, and voices shouting for an ambulance and the police. And Maggie eventually stopped screaming. Someone was saying soothing words to her and asking if she was hurt. Such was her shock, that she couldn't even check herself for injuries.

She soon became aware of Sam's body being lifted from hers by a kind-faced paramedic. Then another paramedic checked her for injuries and declared her fine. But she wasn't fine. Sam was dead. And he had died by throwing himself in front of a bullet which had been aimed at her.

The next few hours were a blur. Maggie was taken to the hospital and checked over again. Questions were asked of her, but she could only give her name and address. Her mind had shut down. It couldn't cope with any more shocks. A kind nurse placed her in an open room with upholstered chairs and sat her down.

Hot drinks were placed in her hands at various times, but she forgot to drink them.

Her mind began to work again. Where was Sam now? What would happen to his body? Jake! She should phone Jake. Or had someone already phoned him?

Thoughts about Jake brought her out of her stupor. She had to do something.

Maggie went over to the nearest reception desk and asked about Sam, and what would happen to him now.

The nurse looked as if she wasn't going to answer for a moment, but then she said, "He's okay. The bullet passed right through his shoulder. He's one lucky man."

Maggie put her hand on the desk to steady herself. "He's still alive?"

The nurse nodded. "He lost a lot of blood, but he's going to be okay. He's asleep at the moment."

"His son, Jake, has anyone phoned him?"

"Yes. I phoned him. I found Mr Ward's phone, and his son was listed. He's on his way." The nurse gave Maggie a small smile. "Jake asked about you, and I told him you were fine. The police still want to talk to you. They couldn't get any sense out of you earlier."

"Right. Okay. I'm not sure what to tell them." Or where to begin, Maggie thought. But wouldn't it be better to tell them everything right from the beginning? "I can talk to them now."

"They've had to leave suddenly. A fight's broken out in a pub." She rolled her eyes. "Vampires, would you believe it? They can't handle their beer. The police will be back soon. There are a couple of officers on the outside door who are checking everyone who enters. It's not often we get a shooting around here."

Knowing there were police at the door helped alleviate Maggie's fears a little.

"Is there anything I can get for you?" the nurse asked. "There's a vending machine just down the corridor if you're hungry. And you can clean yourself up in the bathroom."

Maggie winced as she became aware of the dried blood on her clothes. "Thank you. Would it be okay if I wait for Jake? And I'd like to see Sam too."

"Of course. The waiting room is quiet, so you can have a lie-down if you need to. A bit of sleep will help you."

Maggie didn't think she could sleep. But she was wrong. After a weak cup of tea, and a feeble attempt at cleaning herself up, her body decided it needed to shut down for a bit. Maggie made herself as comfortable as possible on the padded seats, and rested her eyes. She kept a tight hold on her handbag.

She was jolted awake later by her phone buzzing in her handbag. She forced herself into a sitting position, her body twitching with pain in various areas, and took her phone from her bag. It was Oscar.

"Mum! Where have you been? I've been trying to get hold of you all last night, and this morning."

Morning? Maggie glanced at the one window in the room. The bright light of a new day was visible outside. Had she really slept through the night?

Her voice was groggy as she replied, "Oscar, hello. Is everything okay?"

He laughed, "As if you didn't know! Where are you now? On your way to see me, I assume. You could have just sent me a text to let me know. I've taken the day off work, so I'll be in when you get here."

Maggie rubbed her forehead in an effort to wake her brain up. "You're not making any sense. I'm not on my way to see you at all."

"But the T-shirt? That one with the hedgehog on it." He laughed again. "You and your hedgehogs!"

Fear gripped Maggie. "What T-shirt?"

"That one you sent me last night by special delivery."

Maggie swallowed her fear. "Was there a note with the T-shirt?"

"You should know; you sent it."

"Oscar, listen to me carefully. I didn't send that T-shirt. I can't go into details now, but someone has been playing nasty tricks on me using T-shirts with hedgehogs on them."

There was silence on the other end of the phone.

"Oscar? Oscar! Are you still there?"

"What do you mean, nasty tricks? Who would do that to you? Give me their names." There was anger in his voice.

"It doesn't matter. I'm dealing with it. Is there a message with the T-shirt? Maybe on it."

"Mum, what's going on? Where are you?"

"Oscar," Maggie's voice was stern now. "Tell me about the T-shirt. It's vitally important. Is there a message?"

"Yes. There's a speech bubble coming from the hedgehog's mouth. It says, 'Surprise' with three exclamation marks after it. Underneath that, it says, 'I'm coming to see you tomorrow' with five exclamation marks after those words. There's no note to say who sent it, but I assumed it was you because of your obsession with hedgehogs."

Maggie closed her eyes and willed herself to think clearly. An idea came to her. She opened her eyes, and said, "Oscar, you need to get out of your house now. Right now."

"But—"

"No! Listen to me. Get out now. Do you remember that car museum Dad took us to when you were nine?"

"Yes, but—"

"Go there now. Wait in the car park. I'll meet you there. I'm in Whitby, so it'll take me an hour or so. Wait for me there. Okay?"

"Whitby? Why are you there? What's going on?"

"I'll tell you everything when I see you. Oscar, go right now." Her voice trembled. "I love you so much. Do as I say. Please."

She expected him to argue with her again, but he didn't. He said, "I'm walking out of the house now. Love you too, Mum."

Maggie blinked away the threat of tears. The fear which had been a constant companion for days was replaced with anger. The killer was after her son now. That was unacceptable.

Maggie would give her life to protect Oscar. And, she realised, it might just come to that.

Chapter 41

There was a different nurse on reception, and Maggie quickly asked her about Sam. The nurse told her the patient was with his son, but she wouldn't give any further information until Maggie confirmed she was a relative. Maggie gave her a tight smile and walked swiftly away before the nurse asked who she was, and why she was there.

Maggie knew the police still wanted to talk to her, but she didn't have time to wait for them. She had to get out of the hospital immediately. There were a couple of young police officers near the exit doors, but they were busy examining the bags of two elderly women who were coming in. The women looked outraged, and loudly expressed their feelings. It was enough of a commotion to allow Maggie to sneak out without being noticed.

Once away from the hospital, Maggie checked her handbag to make sure the stash of money was still there and hadn't been stolen in the night by a devious thief. Thankfully, the money was still there. She didn't have time to catch a train, so a taxi would be needed.

As she phoned for a taxi, Maggie was aware that the killer could be watching her right now. She hoped they were. She'd rather the killer was watching her than Oscar. Her fear and worries had been replaced by a fierce determination to protect her child.

The taxi arrived, and Maggie was soon heading away from Whitby. The driver was delighted about the big fare he was going to receive, but thankfully, he was the silent type and didn't say a word until they pulled into the museum car park fifty-five minutes later.

Maggie's good manners got the better of her, and she included a generous tip for the driver.

The taxi drove off, leaving Maggie in a deserted car park. Her heart sank when she realised why it was deserted. The museum had closed, and years ago going by the dilapidated look of the building. Maggie was hoping the car park and building would be full of visitors in case the killer turned up. But then, tourists hadn't stopped the killer shooting at her in Whitby.

Where was Oscar? Had he seen how empty the car park was and parked somewhere else?

Was he stuck in traffic?

Had the killer caught up with him and—

No! She would not entertain that thought.

Oscar would be here very soon. Then she'd tell him everything. And they would go to the police, and they would soon discover who had shot Sam. There would be CCTV to help them, wouldn't there? Maybe the police were already working on it right now.

Maggie forced herself to think one comforting thought after another.

Sam. He was okay. And he'd risked his life to save her. He wasn't the killer after all. She could trust him. She hoped.

She was so lost in her self-comforting thoughts, that she didn't notice the vehicle coming into the car park.

Until it stopped right at her side.

Chapter 42

Maggie held back a scream as she became aware of the vehicle at her side. Her fear was quickly replaced with relief when she recognised the white van.

The passenger window lowered. From the driver's side, Jake called over, "Get in! Quickly."

"But Oscar? I'm waiting for my son."

"He's not coming. Get in." Jake glanced at the rear-view mirror nervously.

"How do you know he's not coming? Where is he?"

Jake was still looking at the mirror.

"Jake! Where's my son?"

"Somewhere safe. Get in right now! We can't stay here."

Despite her reservations, Maggie got in the van. Jake sped out of the car park before she'd even closed the door.

"Slow down!" Maggie cried out. "I haven't even put my seat belt on yet. Where's Oscar? Tell me."

Jake roared down the road, his attention kept going to the rear-view mirror. "He's staying with a trusted contact. He's not far away. It wasn't safe for him to meet you here." He finally looked at her. "That was a terrible meeting place, you know. A deserted car park in the middle of nowhere. What were you thinking?"

Maggie tensed. "It was all I could think of at the time. I'm not used to arranging urgent meetings with my son because a killer is after us. Where exactly is Oscar? And how did he get there?"

Jake concentrated on the road. He was still going at a ridiculously fast pace. "I heard you talking to him."

"How?"

Not looking the slightest bit embarrassed, he said, "There's a tracking device on that phone Dad gave you."

"But your dad said there wasn't." Fresh suspicion about Sam filled Maggie.

"There wasn't. I put it there last night at the hospital while you were sleeping. You don't half make a racket when you snore. Anyway, the device records your calls too. I phoned Oscar after you'd spoken to him, and arranged for him to go somewhere safe. I don't know why you had to leave the hospital like that. Why didn't you talk to me before rushing off like an idiot?"

"Hey! Don't talk to me like that. And don't tell me what to do when it comes to my son."

Jake's nostrils flared, but he clamped his lips together. The van went even faster, and Maggie was thrown to one side as they squealed around a bend.

"Slow down!" Maggie ordered him. "Does Oscar know what's going on?"

"Nope."

"He must be worried sick about me."

Jake gave her a half-shrug as if that didn't matter.

"Are you taking me to him now?"

"Yep."

"And then what?"

He looked her way. "What do you mean?" He looked back at the road.

"There's a killer after me. And my son. I have to do something about it. Have the police been in touch with you? Have they spoken to your dad? How is he, by the way?"

"Thanks for asking." Jake's voice dripped with sarcasm. "Dad's fine. But he could have died because of you." He blinked rapidly, and Maggie could see how Jake was trying to keep a tight hold of his emotions. That didn't excuse how rude he was being, though.

Maggie said, "I did speak to the nurses about your dad. I knew he was okay. And I'm sorry he got shot. I'm sorry I got him involved in this mess. And you too."

Jake gave her a dismissive sniff in reply which could have meant anything.

Maggie carried on. "Take me to Oscar, then I'll speak to the police. You can go back to the hospital and take care of your dad."

"No."

Maggie sighed. "You sound like your dad. What does 'no' mean?"

"I'm taking you to the safe house. You'll stay there until I sort everything out. I know what to do."

"But the police—"

He shot her a look. "I don't know why you keep thinking the police will magically deal with this. They haven't yet, have they? Mum's trying her best, I know she is. But she hasn't found anything out yet. So, I'm going to find the person responsible. I'm getting closer to finding out who it is."

"What do you mean?"

He glanced at the rear-view mirror before answering. "That old woman who lives in the murder house on your street, she knows something. I'm going to talk to her." His focus went back on the mirror. "Someone's following us. They're getting closer. Hold on."

"To what?" Maggie grabbed the handle of the door as the van shot forward.

Jake raced along the winding roads as if the devil were after them. Maggie was thrown from side to side with the breath being knocked from her.

Jake suddenly turned to the left and headed down a narrow country lane.

Maggie bumped in her seat. "Are they still behind us?"

"I think I've lost them."

"Then slow down!"

"I can't." More than half his attention was on the rear-view mirror.

Maggie screamed, "Watch out! There's something on the road!" Foolishly, she pulled on the steering wheel.

She was too rough with the wheel.

The van skidded, and veered to the left. Jake fought to get control of it, but failed.

The van sped off the road and towards a thick oak tree.

Maggie didn't know who screamed the loudest as they rushed towards the tree. She braced herself for the inevitable collision.

CRASH!

There was the sound of crunching metal, and then deafening silence as Maggie registered what had just happened.

"Jake?" She looked his way. The young man's head was resting on the dashboard. "Jake? JAKE!"

He didn't move.

There was a sound behind them. Maggie half turned in her seat. An unfamiliar vehicle had pulled up behind the van.

Chapter 43

Now what? Hadn't she been through enough?

Maggie tapped Jake gently on the shoulder, and whispered, "Jake, are you okay? Are you still alive?" She moved her head closer to his and was relieved to hear him breathing. He was alive. For now.

Whoever was in the car behind then turned their engine off.

Maggie opened the glovebox and frantically searched for a weapon of some sort. She wouldn't go down without a fight.

Ah! That would do. She took the can of de-icer from the glovebox and released her seat belt. She gave the can a shake. There was enough liquid inside to cause damage to someone. She didn't like the idea of squirting it at someone, but she didn't like the idea of dying either.

Should she get out? Or wait for the person behind to approach her?

She waited.

Nothing happened.

Maggie tilted the rear-view mirror until she could see the car behind more clearly.

She let out a startled gasp when she saw the driver. What was he doing here?

Still holding the de-icer, she got out of the van and walked over to the car. She knocked on the driver's window. The sight of his pale face and closed eyes made her pulse race. Was he still alive?

The driver opened his eyes, focused them on her, and managed a weak smile. The driver's window lowered. Sam said, "Fancy meeting you here. What's with the de-icer? Are you expecting frost?" He winced at the last words as if speaking them had caused him pain.

Maggie said, "What are you doing here? You're supposed to be in hospital." She pointed the can at his shoulder. "You're bleeding through that bandage! Get back to hospital right now."

"I don't think I can," he replied weakly. "I've run out of energy."

"Why are you here? Did the killer turn up at the hospital?"

"No. I wanted to see where Jake was going. As soon as he knew you'd left the hospital, he went chasing after you. And I went after him. He's so reckless sometimes."

"He's reckless? I wonder where he gets it from?" She put the de-icer on the ground, and placed the back of her hand on Sam's forehead. "You're burning up. I'm phoning for an ambulance. Jake needs one too."

"No, I don't. I'm fine. Totally fine. What's wrong with Jake? He looks okay to me."

Maggie turned around to see Jake weaving his way unsteadily towards them. There was an eye-watering gash on his forehead. His floppy hair was matted with blood.

"Get back in that van," Maggie ordered him. "No, in fact, get in this car with your dad. Then I can keep an eye on you both."

Jake gave Sam a friendly wave. "Hiya! What are you doing here?" His words were slurred. "Where did you get that car from? I don't like it."

Sam grimaced as he forced his words out. "I stole it from the hospital car park."

Jake began to giggle like a little boy. "Stole it. You're in big trouble." He winced. "I feel weird."

Maggie put a firm hand on Jake's shoulder. "Stop talking, and get in the car."

"You can't tell me what to do," Jake became belligerent. "You made me crash. Dad, did you see me crash? It was her fault. She grabbed the wheel." He frowned at Maggie. "Why did you grab the wheel?"

"Erm." Maggie looked away from his accusing stare. "There was a creature on the road."

"What sort of a creature?" Jake jabbed her shoulder roughly.

Maggie pushed his finger away. "It was a hedgehog."

Jake looked momentarily stunned. "You're kidding me."

She gave him a direct look. "I'm not. The poor little thing was in the middle of the road. You were going to run over him."

Jake's expression darkened. "Hedgehogs. Hedgehogs! Stupid hedgehogs! I should have run it over! All this trouble is down to those evil, spiky creatures." He looked back at the road. "Where is it? I'm going to kill it right now. And then I'm going to hunt down his family and kill them too. Then I'm going to your house, and I'm going to find those monsters in your garden—"

He didn't finish his threat because he collapsed, quite elegantly, into a bush behind him. Maggie was relieved to see his chest still moving.

"Sam, I'm going to put—" Maggie stopped talking because Sam had passed out too.

"Great. Just great," Maggie said to herself. "What am I supposed to do now?"

Chapter 44

The killer drank a latte while watching Maggie and her new friends. Wasn't modern technology marvellous? That drone which was providing live footage was amazing. The killer had thoroughly enjoyed seeing all the different emotions on Maggie's face. Fear was the best one, by far.

The killer looked closer at the image. That look of determination on Maggie's face wasn't pleasing at all. It didn't suit Maggie's pathetic face.

The killer put the latte down. Time for the last part of the plan. Goodbye, Maggie Kelburn.

Chapter 45

Maggie took control of the situation.

First, she phoned for an ambulance, and said there were two casualties. Whilst she was on the phone, she alternated between looking at Jake and Sam. They were both still out for the count, but they were breathing steadily.

After the ambulance had been sorted out, Maggie phoned the nearest garage about the van. The man she spoke to was very helpful, and he said he'd be there soon.

During both phone calls, Maggie realised she didn't know where she was. But both times, the person she was speaking to said they could track her position from the GPS on her phone. She didn't know whether to be worried about that or relieved. Sam had told her the phone he'd given her was safe, but it couldn't be that safe if she could easily be tracked down. But there again, Jake did say he'd put a device on her phone.

Well, there was nothing she could do about that. She checked on her casualties again. She did linger a bit too long over Sam, and couldn't help but gaze at his handsome, yet deathly pale, face. She wasn't sure she could trust him, but she wanted to.

The ambulance arrived quickly, and Maggie was happy to step back and let them take over. She did tell them the car had been stolen from the hospital car park, and perhaps they could let the owner know.

Maggie declined the offer to go with Sam and Jake to the hospital, but she asked the man who turned up for the van if he could give her a lift to his garage. She wanted to get a taxi but didn't want to wait for one on her own in the middle of a deserted country lane.

The man from the garage was happy to give her a lift, particularly as Maggie paid him upfront to keep the van at his garage for a few days.

Maggie was aware she was burning through her stash of money, but it couldn't be helped. She had to get to Leeds as soon as possible. She had a plan, and she wasn't going to deviate from it.

Chapter 46

Hours later, Maggie slapped her hand on the reception desk, and announced loudly, "I'm not leaving this station until I speak to DCI Dexter!"

"Madam, please lower your voice. And refrain from vandalising the desk. I've already told you DCI Dexter isn't here at the moment."

"I know you did. But you won't tell me when he's back." Maggie was tempted to hit the desk again, but she'd hurt her hand the last time she'd done it. And she was a bit embarrassed at being so forceful. It wasn't in her nature at all, but neither was running away from a murderer.

The officer gave Maggie a hard look, and then consulted the screen in front of him.

"I'm sorry," Maggie said. "I didn't mean to shout. I'm having a horrible day. A horrible week, in fact."

The officer gave her a sympathetic smile. "So am I. My cat died. She's been with me for over ten years. Always there for me at the end of the day. Such a loyal and devoted companion."

Maggie's suppressed emotions burst forth. Tears suddenly streamed down her cheeks. "Your cat? Oh no. I'm so sorry. You poor thing. And here I am, shouting at you and attacking your desk. I'm so very, very sorry."

The officer's smile was wobbly. "Thank you. Wait here. DCI Dexter is due back soon. I'll see if he's turned up early."

The officer went through a door behind him. A few seconds later, a hard-faced DCI Dexter came through the door.

Maggie was wiping her eyes at this stage, and desperately willing her earlier confidence to come back. This wasn't the time to be weepy and weak.

"Can I help you?" DCI Dexter said coldly.

The icy tone in his voice was like a catalyst. Maggie's anger and determination hit her like a speeding train.

"I don't know. Can you help me? Will you help me? Isn't that your job?" Maggie glowered at him. "Or are you going to dismiss me like you did last time?"

"There's no need to shout, Ms Kelburn. If you continue to raise your voice, I will have no option but to ask you to leave the station."

"You will do no such thing," Maggie said, suddenly calm. "I reported a murder to you a few days ago. In good faith, thinking you would take it seriously. I was wrong. Since that report, I have been on the run. To Morecambe and Whitby. I was shot at on the steps leading to the Abbey."

"Shot at? Ms Kelburn, will you—"

"I haven't finished talking. I was shot at. Obviously, they missed. The blood on my clothes is not mine."

"Ms Kelburn, if you will just—"

"I still haven't finished. My son received a message from the person who had tried to kill me. Because his life is now in danger, he's in a safe place. I don't even know where he is. And I've paid an eye-watering amount of money to get a taxi to this station." She gave him a grim look. "And I haven't had a shower in ages. Or changed my clothes. I stink to high heaven."

DCI Dexter nodded at her last comment. "I am aware of the latter fact. But I have smelled worse. Ms Kelburn, come with me into a private office. I want all the details. Let me get you a hot drink. Would you like something to eat?"

"I'm not hungry, but a drink would be nice. Thank you."

Maggie followed the inspector through the door at the side of the reception desk, and into a private office.

He pulled a chair out for her. "Please, take a seat. Tea or coffee?"

"Tea. Thank you." Maggie didn't know why she kept saying thank you. "Milk, no sugar."

He gave her a nod, and left the room.

Maggie took the opportunity to look around the room. She was expecting to see a mirror on one wall like she'd seen on TV shows. A two-way mirror so police officers could spy on her, and make comments. But there wasn't a mirrored wall.

DCI Dexter returned with a mug of dark brown tea in one hand, and a chocolate muffin on a plate in his other. He set the items on the table, and nodded at the muffin. "Just in case you get peckish," he said as he sat down. "Tell me about the shooting, and why you were on the run."

Maggie began. She kept taking sips of tea and nibbles of the muffin during her talk. The inspector listened intently and took notes.

When Maggie got to the bit about Sam being shot, he took a sharp intake of breath but didn't say anything. He did say something when she told him about Jake being injured when the van crashed.

"Excuse me a moment," he said as he abruptly rose from his chair. He swiftly left the room but came back two minutes later. He returned to his seat, and said, "Continue, please."

Maggie did so, and ended with, "And here I am. Not knowing where my son is. Unable to return home. And a murderer is out to get me."

DCI Dexter nodded, and said, "We can deal with all of those things. Your safety is a priority, so first of all—"

He didn't get any further than that, because the door was flung open. A red-faced Ingrid stood there shooting daggers of hate at Maggie.

DCI Dexter leapt to his feet. "PC Ward, you are not needed here. Please, leave the room."

Ingrid completely ignored him. She aimed her words at Maggie. "You! What have you done? My son is in the hospital because of you! He could have died because of you! And his father was shot because of you! You awful—"

Her insults were cut short as DCI Dexter firmly manoeuvred her out of the office. Maggie heard mutterings and shouts as the door closed. Mutterings from the inspector, but shouts coming from Ingrid. Maggie understood Ingrid's anger, but none of this was Maggie's fault. Was it?

DCI Dexter returned to the room. "I apologise for PC Ward's behaviour."

"It's okay. I'd be angry too in her shoes."

"Yes, but she should know better. Ms Kelburn, you can leave everything to us now. You've given us a lot of information which we didn't have before, especially concerning the name of your neighbour who was murdered. That will help us a lot. In the meantime, I'd like you to stay at a local hotel, at our expense." He handed her a card. "I've already phoned them to say you're on the way. You'll be safe there."

"Thank you. What about my son?"

"We'll track him down. You'll soon be reunited with him." He gave her a reassuring smile. "You don't have to worry about anything."

"That's easy for you to say," Maggie replied. "But I've done nothing but worry."

He held the door open for her, and said, "I apologise for the treatment you received from us earlier. We should have taken the matter more seriously. I've put my phone number on the back of that card. Ring me if you need to, for any reason. Okay?"

"Okay. Thanks." Maggie gave him a small smile. He was being very helpful, and she hoped he was being genuine.

Maggie was shown out of the room and back to the reception area. As the door closed behind her, she heard DCI Dexter say to someone, "Hey, remember those protected person murders a few months back? Yeah. We've finally got a connection."

A connection? What did that mean? And why hadn't the DCI told her about a connection?

Maggie sighed quietly. Why couldn't anyone be truthful with her?

Chapter 47

Maggie had every intention of going to the hotel which the inspector had told her about, having a long shower, and then letting the police get on with things. But she couldn't just sit and wait for things to happen. She had to do something.

So, she did.

She got a taxi back to the street where she lived. She didn't head to her own house, though. Instead, she knocked firmly on the door of number forty-eight. She knew the old woman was in because Maggie had seen her looking out of the window when Maggie's taxi had pulled up.

Maggie opened the letterbox in the door, and shouted through it, "I know you're in there! I'm not leaving until I talk to you. I've nowhere else to go. I can stay here for hours!" She knocked on the door again for good measure.

The door was abruptly opened. The old woman was red with fury. "Clear off! I don't want to talk to you."

"Tough. I want to talk to you."

"Tough right back at you! I'm not saying another word." She tried to close the door. Maggie slammed her hand on it. The woman threatened, "I'll phone the police."

Maggie didn't miss the uncertainty in the woman's voice as she mentioned the police. Maggie took a chance. "Go ahead. Phone them. Let them know you only moved into this street a few days ago."

"That's a lie. I've been here for weeks."

"You haven't. I would have seen you." Maggie lowered her voice. "The man who lived here was murdered in the living room. I saw it happen."

She expected the woman to be shocked at that, but the old woman tutted, and said, "You'd better come in. I don't want everyone on the street knowing my business."

Maggie went inside, and into the living room. It was sparsely decorated with cheap-looking furniture. She immediately noticed the carpet was new. There weren't any items to make the room look cosy and homely, apart from half a dozen silver-framed photos on the mantelpiece.

Maggie jumped as a hissing sound shot out behind her. The woman was spraying Maggie with air freshener, and the cloud of perfumed air made Maggie splutter.

Maggie flapped a hand to clear the cloud. "Hey! Stop that."

"You stink," the woman informed her. "I don't want you stinking up my house. You didn't smell this bad the other day. Doesn't your shower work? Haven't you paid your water bill?" She went over to the window and opened it.

Maggie said, "I've been on the run. On account of witnessing the murder of the man who lived here." She moved over to the armchair.

"Don't move! I don't want your filthy clothes staining my cushions. What is that muck on your jacket and top?"

"Dried blood. I tried to clean it off."

"You've done a terrible job. It looks a right mess." The woman scurried out of the room, and then returned with a black bin liner. She opened it out, and then carefully placed it over the armchair so that every inch was covered. She said to Maggie, "You can sit down now. Don't expect a drink. You won't be staying that long."

Maggie was past being offended by now. She pointed at the carpet, and said, "This is new. It must have been put here by whoever killed that man."

The old woman settled herself in the opposite chair, but didn't say anything.

Maggie continued. "I don't know if I should say this or not, but the man who was killed was called William Phelps. That wasn't his real name. He was in a person protection scheme. I don't know why. But someone who's been helping me look into his death, told me you know something." The last part wasn't exactly true, but Maggie wasn't going to tell the woman that.

The woman didn't flinch, twitch or deny anything Maggie said.

Maggie glanced towards the framed photos. They showed three men getting older in each photo. "Are those your sons? They have a look of you about them."

"What if they are? What's that got to do with you?"

"I've got a son. He's called Oscar. He looks more like his dad than me. Because of the murder of William Phelps, my son's life has been put in danger. Apparently, he's in a safe house somewhere. I don't know where. And it scares me because I'm assuming William Phelps thought this was a safe house too. And look what happened to him."

Maggie paused, expecting to see a reaction on the woman's face. But there wasn't one. Maggie was beginning to suspect the woman had a heart of stone.

"Since I saw that murder, it's been one horrific thing after another for me. I can't even go into my house," Maggie explained. "I haven't showered or changed for days. I feel grubby and exhausted. But I don't care."

"That's obvious," the woman said with a sniff.

"I don't care, because my only concern is my son." She looked again at the photos. "I'm assuming you love your sons and would do anything to protect them."

"Perhaps," the woman relented. "But they're adults. They can look after themselves. If your son's got himself in danger, then he should sort it out himself. If he can't do that, then you've not done a good job of bringing him up properly."

Her harsh words made Maggie burst into laughter. "You could be right. There aren't any books on being a mother, are there? Apart from those ridiculous ones from so-called experts who set impossible rules. I've done my best, but I've had to learn on the job. And it doesn't matter how old Oscar is; he'll always be my little boy. And I'll always be there to protect him. Hopefully."

The woman's sharp eyes narrowed. "Hopefully? What does that mean?"

Maggie gave her a dismissive shrug. "Someone's trying to kill me."

"Why? What have you done?"

"Nothing. Apart from seeing that murder and reporting it to the police. Well, I had to. It's what any decent person would do."

The woman's face twisted this way and that way as if she was wondering what to say next.

Maggie leaned forward on her knees. "I need your help. The police are keeping something from me. They said they would deal with this murder thing, but I'm not convinced. I have to keep my son safe. No matter what."

The woman nodded. "I can appreciate that." She looked at the photos of her sons, and then let out a resigned sigh. "Okay. I can tell you something, but if the police come after me, I'll deny speaking to you. Okay?"

Maggie nodded in reply.

"I did move here a few days ago. You're right about that. I don't know about any murder taking place here, and even if I had, I still would have moved in. I need the money, you see. My lads have all been to university. I know they could have taken loans out to help them, but I couldn't let them. I told them their dad had a couple of life policies in place, and that I was using money from the policies to help them. This was after their dad passed away."

"I'm sorry about your husband."

"I'm not. I hated him. Left me with nothing but bruises and debts. But my lads don't know that. Be quiet while I tell you everything. I had a friend of a friend who knew how I could get money with no questions asked. All I had to do was move into empty houses for a while. The houses could be anywhere. I would be there for weeks, months or years. I don't take anything with me apart from a few belongings like my photos. The houses are always furnished."

"Why would someone want you to do that?"

"What did I say about you being quiet? Have you got ears made of cloth? Are you one of those who constantly interrupts? You look the type who does that."

"Sorry," Maggie mumbled.

"I should think so. I don't know why someone would want me to do it. And I don't care. Maybe they want a house to be occupied. They pay me well, and they give me a name I should use when I move to a new place, and a backstory too, if I need it." She folded her arms. "You're judging me. I can see it in your eyes."

"Sorry. It's just that I don't understand why you would do this. You must know it's for dodgy reasons."

"Of course I do! I'm not stupid. But they pay me good money. Really good money. And that money helped my lads through university. And it gave them a deposit on their homes. And now the oldest has got a couple of lads of his own. I like spoiling my grandkids. With a bit of luck, they'll be going to university too."

Maggie couldn't keep quiet. "But a man was murdered here. Right in this room. And you're working with criminals to cover this up. It's not right."

"I didn't kill him! And who are you to judge how I make money? It's none of your business!"

"It is! I'm right in the middle of it all."

Maggie and the old woman stared at each other in defiance.

The woman suddenly sank back in the chair. "I know the money I'm getting isn't from legal sources. But I've come to terms with it. I am sorry you've got involved with whoever is paying me."

"Who's paying you?"

"I don't know. I always get paid in cash. And they always contact me by an unknown number. Even if I did tell the police about how I came to live here, I don't have any evidence to prove it." Her face became stricken. "If I did tell the police, they'd think I had something to do with the murder. They'd lock me up. My sons would be so ashamed. I'd never see my grandkids again."

Maggie felt a surge of sympathy. "I won't tell the police, but they might turn up here anyway. I don't suppose the man who lived here left anything behind? Anything that could help me?"

The woman tapped her chin. "There is something. I don't know whether it will help or not. But when I was told to move in here, I turned up a bit early. The keys to the new homes are usually left in a bin or something, but I got here while a man was putting them in the green bin. He was on his phone. I heard him say something about the man who lived here before me. What was it he said? Something about a jewellery theft, and that the final witness had been sorted out."

"Oh? That's interesting. Maybe William Phelps witnessed the jewellery theft. If it was in a shop, he could have been a customer or a member of staff." She pulled a face. "It seems a bit extreme to kill someone for stolen jewellery."

"It depends how much money was involved, and who was stealing it. But I didn't get the impression the man was that kind of a witness. Oh, I wish I could remember what the man on the phone said. It was only a few days ago. But I think the man who lived here was involved in the theft in another way. Almost like he—" She suddenly screamed.

Maggie shot to her feet. "What? What is it?"

The woman pointed to the window behind Maggie.

A face was looking in at them.

Chapter 48

The face belonged to a woman with hazel eyes. Her hair was long, and light blue with orange and yellow streaks. The woman caught Maggie's eye and gave her an enthusiastic wave.

"Who the heck is that?" the old woman asked. She clutched her chest. "Is it the murderer? Have you led the murderer right to my house?"

"It's my neighbour, Carmella. She's harmless." Maggie couldn't help adding, "The murderer has already been in this house once. They know you live here now."

The woman stood up and pulled her cardigan around her more tightly. "There's no need to remind me. I'm going to rethink my future career plans. It might be time to retire. I'll see you out."

"Thanks for talking to me."

"I didn't have a choice." The woman put her hand over her nose. "Do everyone a favour and have a bath soon."

"I'll try. Is there anything else you can tell me? About that man who lived here?"

"No, that's as much as I know. I'll have to open all the windows to get your stench out. Hurry up and get out." She made shooing motions with her hands but kept her distance as she followed Maggie out of the room.

Maggie left the house and was immediately pulled into a hug by Carmella. Her comforting familiar smell of roses almost caused Maggie to burst into tears. If Carmella noticed the whiff coming from Maggie, she didn't say anything. And she didn't release Maggie from her embrace for a full minute.

When she did release her, Carmella put her hands on the sides of Maggie's face, and said, "I thought you were dead. My dear, dear, wonderful Maggie. I thought I'd never see your lovely face again."

"Dead? Why would you think that?"

"I got a text telling me that." Carmella pulled a phone from somewhere within the colourful voluminous dress she was wearing. She always wore such dresses, and Maggie often thought of Carmella as a butterfly in human form.

"That's strange," Carmella said as she frowned at her phone. "The message has gone, but it was definitely there." She scrolled through her messages. "How odd."

"Was there a name for the sender?"

Carmella gave her a direct look. "Yes. It was from the police. Maggie, my blood turned to ice, pure ice, when I got that message. It said there had been an attempted break-in at your house, and you'd tried to intervene, but had been killed in the process." Her eyes filled with tears. "I actually felt my heart break. I truly did."

Maggie put her arm around Carmella's shoulders. "I'm okay. Just about. I don't know why someone sent you that message, but something terrible has happened recently."

"Oi! You two! Do your talking somewhere else," the old woman shouted from the door of number forty-eight. She gave them a filthy look before slamming the door shut.

Carmella said, "Who's that? Where did that Scottish man go?"

"You remember him? The Scottish man?" Maggie led Carmella away from the house and along the street towards the main road.

"Yes. I saw him in his garden once. I came to this house to ask if he knew about your break-in; that's why I was looking through the window. I did knock, but there was a lot of shouting going on inside. I recognised your voice."

"I was getting angry somewhat. When did you see the Scottish man?"

"A few weeks ago in the back garden. I could only see the top of his ginger head, so I couldn't see his aura. You know how I like to see a person's aura."

Maggie nodded. "How do you know he was Scottish?"

"I heard him on his phone. He was ordering a takeaway. Indian, by the sounds of it. I shouted a hello over to him, but I don't think he heard me. Maggie, where did he go? And who's that grumpy woman? I got a good look at her aura. And it was not pretty, I can tell you. Why are we going this way? I want to go home and make you a strong cup of herbal tea. You look like you need one. Did you really have a break-in?"

"No, I didn't. But we can't go to our homes, not my home anyway."

She stopped talking as a taxi pulled up right next to them. A figure shot out of it and dashed over to Carmella. He pulled her into a fierce hug, and yelled, "You're alive! You're alive!"

"Oscar, hello," Maggie said as she tried to get her son's attention.

He looked her way but didn't let Carmella go. "Mum? What are you doing here?"

"It's complicated. Let Carmella go. You're squashing her."

"But I thought she was dead," He released Carmella a fraction and gazed adoringly into her eyes. "I thought you were dead."

Carmella politely pulled herself free and smoothed down her dress. "I'm very much alive, Oscar. I did have a touch of indigestion yesterday. But a couple of cups of mint tea soon sorted that out. How are you? How's your business doing? Are you any closer to saving the planet yet?"

Oscar was still gazing at her and seemed incapable of talking.

Maggie roughly pulled him into a tight embrace. "I'm so pleased to see you. I thought you were in a safe house."

His voice was muffled. "I was, but I left. I had to when I heard Carmella was dead. Mum, you're a bit whiffy."

Maggie released him. "Sorry about the smell. I'll explain why in a bit. Tell me more about Carmella's supposed death. Who told you that?"

"I got a text." He looked at his phone.

"Oh! I got one too," Carmella announced. "But it was about your mum. And the text has magically disappeared."

Oscar frowned. "My message has gone too. That's weird."

Carmella nodded. "Did the message say how I had returned to the spirit realm? Was my alleged death something exciting and highly original? I hope it was."

"You got hit by a bus."

"Oh. How disappointing. What number bus?"

Oscar shrugged. "The text didn't say. I'm so glad you're still alive. Could I give you another hug?"

Carmella stepped to one side. "I don't think that's necessary. But thank you for the offer. Oscar, Maggie, what's going on? What's this about a safe house?"

Maggie didn't answer her. "Oscar, who sent the text?"

"It came from the police. They said I should come here because they wanted to talk to me inside your house, Mum. They didn't say what about."

"That's what my text said too," Carmella said. "I was about to give a talk about the afterlife at the festival when I got the text. I left the festival hall immediately. But all the way here, Maggie, I couldn't feel your spirit nearby. I couldn't sense that you'd passed. I should have known the text was fake." She shook her head sadly. "My psychic abilities are letting me down. My chakras need cleansing."

Maggie was only half listening. A horrific thought suddenly descended on her. "The killer wanted you both here. On this street."

Carmella shrieked. "The killer? Maggie, what are you talking about?"

Oscar said matter-of-factly, "Mum saw the man in number forty-eight being murdered. Then she had to leave her house and make a getaway with a man called Sam Ward. That's what the person in the safe house told me." He gave Maggie a suspicious look. "Who is this Sam Ward anyway? What's his story?"

"It doesn't matter. I'll tell you everything soon. Both of you." Maggie nervously looked left and right, and then over her shoulder. "We have to go. And now. Someone could be watching us."

"A getaway?" Carmella said, her eyes shining with excitement. "I know where we can go. One of my friends has a charming little cottage on the outskirts of York. Off the beaten track, as they say. I stayed there once, but I can't remember how I got there. But I could use my pendulum to guide us." She reached into one of her hidden pockets.

"Would your friend mind if we stayed there?" Maggie asked. The back of her neck was prickling with fear. "We have to go now."

"Sonia wouldn't mind at all. This is weird, but she actually offered me the cottage before I left the festival abruptly." Carmella threw her hands up in frustration. "Oh! Of course! That's why Sonia said that to me. Those were her parting words before I raced off. Her sixth sense must have told her I would need a safe place to stay very soon. She's an excellent psychic. Obviously much better than me."

"Don't be hard on yourself," Oscar said as he put his arm around Carmella's shoulders. "You're wonderful. Amazing. And I'm so glad you're not dead."

"Me too." Carmella shrugged herself free. "I've got Sonia's address in my house somewhere. I'll go and get it."

Before Maggie could stop her, Carmella hitched up her billowy dress and raced down the street towards her house.

"No!" Maggie screamed. "It's not safe!"

Chapter 49

With surprising speed, Carmella dashed towards her house.

"After her!" Maggie yelled at Oscar. Her son shot off, and Maggie did her best to keep up.

By the time they had reached Carmella's house, she was in the kitchen rifling through a drawer.

Maggie pulled on Carmella's sleeve. "You can't stay here."

"I'm not. I'm looking for Sonia's address. I think I wrote it on the back of a takeaway menu. A pizza one, I think. Won't be a mo."

Maggie wrung her hands together. "Please, hurry."

Carmella gave her a bright smile. "Don't worry. I put a protective light around us as soon as Oscar said you'd seen a murder."

"I'm not sure a protective light will help us." Maggie's heart began to pound in her chest. "Carmella, let's get out of here. There's a hotel we can stay in. The police gave me the address."

Carmella stopped rifling. "The police? The ones who sent me that text?"

"No, not them. The actual police. Let's go to the hotel instead."

Oscar said, "Mum, I don't think we should trust the police. The person at the safe house said the police weren't being helpful. And I don't think you should go to that hotel they suggested. Carmella, what do you think?"

Carmella put her hands on her hips. "I don't know what to think, Oscar. My thoughts are not clear today. There's an unworldly presence on this street. I felt it as soon as I ran along the street just now. I wonder if the spirit of our unfortunate neighbour is trying to get my attention. Let me try and talk to him." She closed her eyes.

Maggie refrained from giving Carmella a firm push towards the open kitchen door. "We don't have time for you to contact the dead. You can try later, and find out who killed him."

Carmella's eye shot open. "It wasn't a pizza menu! I wrote Sonia's address on the back of a Christmas card. One with a cute robin on it. It's in the third drawer down, next to my television in the living room." She clasped her hands together, smiled, and said to the air, "Thank you, psychic ability, for returning to me."

Maggie said, "I'll look for the Christmas card. Oscar, stay here with Carmella, and—"

"Protect her?" Oscar thrust his chest out. "I will do that."

Carmella waved her arms around. "I'm increasing the strength of our protective light."

Maggie shook her head slightly, but not so that Carmella would notice. She loved Carmella, but her friend put too much faith in the spiritual side of life.

Maggie went over to the drawers next to the TV, and pulled open the third one. She sighed in dismay when she saw the piles of Christmas cards inside. She picked a handful up, and quickly discarded the non-robin ones.

It didn't take her that long to find the card which had Sonia's name and address on the back.

Maggie jumped as she felt a hand on her back.

"It's only me," Oscar said. "Do you need any help?"

"No, thanks. I've found it." She waved the card at him. "You're supposed to be protecting Carmella."

"She's having some meditation time in the kitchen, to collect her thoughts." A noise came to them.

Maggie stiffened. "Was that the kitchen door closing?"

"I don't know." Oscar was already running out of the living room.

Maggie raced after him. The kitchen was empty.

"Carmella?" Maggie cried out. "Where are you?"

Oscar pointed to the kitchen window. "She's outside. She's touching something on the washing line."

Maggie swiftly joined Oscar at the window. Carmella was holding on to the edge of a green T-shirt. There was an image of a prickly creature on the T-shirt.

Maggie's hand flew to her mouth.

Oscar quickly took in the situation. He left Maggie's side and rushed outside.

"No! Oscar! Come back! It's not safe." Maggie ran after her son and into the garden.

A gunshot rang out.

Maggie screamed as someone she loved dearly fell to the grass.

Chapter 50

Oscar knelt at Carmella's side. "No! Carmella! No!" He began to sob.

Maggie's eyes stung with tears. She attempted to pull her son away. "We have to get out of here. Pick her up."

Oscar was crying too loudly to hear her, or he was too distraught to hear her. He cradled Carmella's head in his lap and stroked her light blue hair. "I never got the chance to tell you how I feel."

Maggie pulled on his sleeve. He didn't budge.

Carmella's eyes fluttered open. She gave Oscar a gentle smile. "I know how you feel. Alas, we can never be together. We are in different seasons of our lives."

"You're alive!" Oscar cried out. "It's a miracle."

"No, it's a near miss." Carmella pulled herself into a sitting position. She put a hand on her ear and winced. When she pulled her hand free, it was smeared with blood. "Ouch. Whatever went whizzing past my ear has nicked me."

"Let me take care of you." Oscar stood up. He attempted to pick Carmella up, but she pushed his hands away. "I can take care of myself. I just need a plaster, that's all." She stood up, but wobbled on her feet. "Gosh. It seems I'm in a bit of shock. Oscar, would you mind helping me to the kitchen? Thank you."

Oscar put his arm around her shoulders and helped her along.

Maggie urged them to hurry. "Quickly! Before they take another shot at us!"

No one said another word until they were back inside Carmella's kitchen. Carmella quickly bathed her wound, and then put a glittery pink plaster on it.

Carmella pronounced, "All better. Maggie, we need to get out of here immediately. Did you find Sonia's address?"

"I did. I'll phone for a taxi. I'm not sure how safe it is using my phone, but we need to get away from here."

Carmella nodded. "I agree, but we'll take my car. It'll be quicker." She swayed on her feet. "Maggie, could you drive? I'm not feeling myself. I've never been shot at before. My chakras are all over the place, and they weren't in good health before I went outside to see what that strange item was on my washing line. The car keys are by the door."

Maggie nodded in response. She took the keys from the hook. Carmella's car was parked at the bottom of the driveway. They would have to make a run for it and hope the killer wouldn't take another shot at them.

Maggie opened the kitchen door. "Ready? Be as quick as you can." She looked towards Carmella's bright yellow Volkswagen Beetle. It must be the most conspicuous car on the planet. But it was their only option.

Oscar took Carmella's hand, and said, "We should sit in the back. If you're going to faint, let me know, and I'll hold you in my arms."

Carmella gave him an uncertain smile.

"Go!" Maggie shouted.

They were in the car and driving away within thirty seconds. Maggie struggled with the car's gear stick, but that was probably due to her sweaty palms rather than the unfamiliar mechanics of the car.

Maggie had given Oscar the card with Sonia's address on it. She called over her shoulder, "Oscar, tell me where we're going. I know it's on the way to York, so I'll head for the A64."

Through the rear-view mirror, she saw him looking at his phone. Maggie yelled, "No! Don't go on the internet!"

"How else am I supposed to find our way?" he replied.

Carmella picked up on Maggie's meaning. "I don't think it's safe to go online. Whoever sent those texts could have magically put one of those tracking devices on our phones. They will know where we are. Is that right, Maggie?"

Maggie nodded. "It's possible." She didn't add that the killer was most likely following this bright yellow car anyway. She kept looking in the mirror to see if anyone was trailing them. Not that she'd know if they were.

Oscar said, "We should get rid of our phones then no one can track us. I'm going to throw mine out of the window. Carmella, give me yours."

"Oh no, you can't do that, Oscar. Think of the environmental issues. You can't just fling them out of the window."

"Of course I can't!" Oscar sounded mortified. "I should not have said that, Carmella. I'm so sorry."

"It's okay. Is there a recycling centre we can take them to?"

Maggie's hands tightened on the wheel. "We don't have time for that, Carmella. But Oscar's right. We have to get rid of them, or destroy them. Oscar, mine's in my handbag on the front seat."

"But the environment," Carmella began to argue.

Maggie indicated left. "I've got an idea. There's a canal over there. We can drop them in the water. Oscar, when I stop, run out and fling the phones in. If it makes you feel any better, you can come back and fish them out later when..." She didn't know how to end her sentence.

Carmella said with conviction, "When the evil murderer has been caught. Good always triumphs over evil. We'll come back later, get our phones, and then take them to a recycling facility."

Maggie gave her a grateful smile via the mirror. She saw Carmella kissing her phone goodbye before handing it to Oscar.

A few minutes later, Maggie pulled up illegally next to the canal. Oscar jumped out of the car, and with a face full of guilt, dropped their phones into the murky water.

When he got back in the car, he said sadly, "I feel like part of me is missing. How are we going to find our way to Sonia's house now?"

Maggie set off driving again. "Carmella, have you got a map in this car?"

"I have! It's under the passenger seat. I haven't used it in years, but Sonia's village is hundreds of years old. It'll be on the map. Oscar, can you grab it, please?"

Maggie kept watching the traffic behind them, as well as the road in front of her. She couldn't help smiling when she heard Oscar say, "How do I use this map thing? What are all these symbols? This is just stupid. Who even uses maps anyway?"

Carmella gently said, "Oscar, my young friend, the map is upside down. Turn it the right way around, and then we'll start by looking at the index for the street name."

"The index? What do you mean?"

Maggie left them to it while she headed towards the main York Road. Her thoughts were mainly on getting them to safety, but her mind kept going to Sam and Jake. She hoped they were okay. Jake's mum was probably at her son's side by now, or on her way to him. Maggie hoped Sam and Jake wouldn't get involved further in this murder mess. She didn't want to put their lives in danger again. She wouldn't contact them, not until this was over. And she would only contact them to thank them for their help.

With Carmella's help, they found their way to Sonia's cottage. Despite the fading light of the day, Maggie could see the house was as charming as Carmella said it was. A thatched roof cottage with pink roses around the door.

As they got out of the car, Carmella gave Maggie a worried look. She said, "I'd forgotten it was in such an isolated place. We're miles away from the village. Should we stay here? It seemed like a good idea earlier, but I'm not so sure now."

"It'll be fine," Maggie tried to reassure her. She hadn't noticed any cars following them. "Is there a phone inside the house?"

"I don't know." Carmella swallowed nervously. "I hope there is. I don't like the idea of us being shut off from the rest of the world."

"I don't either. But it's getting dark. We can't go looking for anywhere else now."

Carmella gave her a slow nod. "Even so, I feel uneasy. Almost like we're sitting ducks."

Chapter 51

The key to Sonia's house was inside a hollow Buddha statue next to the back door. Carmella opened the door and went inside. Oscar followed. Maggie hesitated while she quickly took in their surroundings, and to check again if anyone had followed them. The little lane they'd driven along was clear of any cars, but the many trees at the side of the lane could be hiding many a suspicious person. Her stomach clenched in fear. What had they got themselves into?

Sonia's house was as colourful as Carmella's, but with the addition of hundreds of crystals. Some were arranged on shelves, others around the fire, and many more on the windowsills. There were even lines of crystals dangling from the ceiling on silver strings.

Carmella noticed Maggie's surprised look, and explained, "Sonia's an expert at crystal energy. As well as being a gifted psychic. She's very popular at the fairs we attend. I should ask her which crystals are good for protection. We could put them near the doors, and in our pockets." She put her hand in one of her pockets. Her face fell. "Oh, I forgot I haven't got my phone anymore"

"Speaking of phones, let's see if we can find one," Maggie said. "I'll check the kitchen and any rooms nearby."

Oscar said, "I'll check the upstairs rooms."

Carmella let out an anguished cry. "Don't bother. I've just remembered that Sonia doesn't have one. She told me when I stayed here before that the phone company wanted to put a telephone post at the end of her lane, but she refused to let them kill a tree just to have a phone installed. She loves trees. She talks to them all the time." Carmella forced a smile on her face. "But maybe she's had one installed since then. Let's look anyway. Let's stay positive."

Oscar nodded. "Yes, we have to stay positive." He moved over to Maggie. "Mum, do you want to tell us what's being going on? What have you gone through? You look like you've aged years."

"Thanks," Maggie mumbled.

He gave her a kind smile. "You still look much younger than you are."

"Good save," she said with a small smile. "Oh! My handbag. I've just remembered Sam put a tracking device in my handbag. He'll know where we are. And if DCI Dexter talks to Sam, Sam will check the device and know where we are."

Carmella punched the air. "Yes! All is well. I'm sure this lovely friend of yours will come to our rescue very soon. Sam? That's his name? He sounds lovely. You must tell me all about him later."

Oscar folded his arms. "I don't like the sound of him. Why did he put a tracking device in your bag? Sounds like a control freak to me."

"He was trying to protect me. He saw the murder footage too. He's gone out of his way to help me." She stopped talking when she saw the suspicion on Oscar's face.

Her son said, "I still don't like the sound of him."

"You will when I give you the full details of what's been going on these last days." Maggie was suddenly aware of an unpleasant smell in the room. It was her. "Erm, Carmella, would it be okay if I have a shower? Would your friend mind?"

"She wouldn't mind at all. There's a guest bedroom at the back of the house. Just up the stairs, and along to the end. It has a silver door. It's a delightful room with a little bathroom. It's where I stayed last time. There might even be a spare pair of pyjamas you could borrow. Fling your clothes out of the bathroom, and I'll put them in the washing machine." She frowned. "If Sonia has a washing machine, that is. She doesn't trust modern contraptions."

Maggie said, "Don't worry about washing my clothes. I'll do it."

Carmella put her hands on Maggie's shoulders and gave her a firm push towards the door which Maggie assumed led to the stairs. Carmella said, "Let us help you. As much as I love you, you're terrible at accepting help from anyone. Go and have a shower. Take your time. Use whatever products you see. Sonia won't mind. And I'll make us a lovely meal from whatever I find. Okay?"

Maggie gave her a nod.

"And after your shower," Carmella continued, "you can tell us about the ordeal you've been through. If we don't find a phone in the house, Oscar and I will have a little stroll down the lane to look for a public phone box."

"Do they still exist?" Oscar asked. "I've never seen one."

"Oh, I'm not sure they do," Carmella said. "But if we don't find one, we'll call on a kind neighbour. Maggie, would you like us to phone your friend Sam, or the police inspector first?"

"Neither," Maggie replied. "I don't want you leaving the house. It's not safe out there. We could have been followed. We should..." She rubbed her forehead. "Sorry, I can't think straight. I'll have a quick shower, and then we'll come up with a plan. Promise me you won't leave this house."

Carmella and Oscar nodded in unison.

Maggie gave them a stern look. "Promise."

"We promise," they said together.

"You'd better both be here when I come back down," Maggie said.

Oscar frowned. "We will. You have to trust us, Mum. We're not going anywhere."

Chapter 52

On weary legs, Maggie headed up the winding stairs and towards a room at the end of the hallway which had a startling bright silver door. The guest room was delightful, even though the shelves were cluttered with more crystals. A relaxing aroma of lavender floated towards Maggie. She gave the comfy-looking bed a longing look. A long sleep sounded like a perfect idea, but she didn't have time for that. Not yet.

The bathroom attached to the bedroom was small, but it had everything Maggie needed. There was a shower cubicle, and inside it was a display of little shampoos and conditioners. Maggie could choose from lavender, rose or honeysuckle. And for a body wash, there was orange, mint or freesia. The bottles had handwritten labels on them. Had Sonia made them herself?

Maggie didn't care whether they were homemade or not, she was just very grateful she could have a shower.

And the shower was amazing. The best one she'd ever had in her life. Or so it seemed. The lotions provided were amazing too, and Maggie found herself lingering in the shower as she washed her hair twice.

She felt like a new woman as she came out of the shower. She went into the room and discovered her grubby discarded clothes had gone. A pair of silver pyjamas were on the bed, along with a fluffy, white dressing gown. A hot drink was on the set of drawers next to the bed, with a note leaning against it.

Maggie read the note and smiled. It was from Carmella:

'We found a little washing machine! Hurrah! I found some camomile tea too. Drink up, you'll feel better for it. Oscar is helping me make something yummy for dinner. See you in the kitchen when you're ready xxx'

Maggie's spirits lifted. She wasn't on her own. She had her dear friend and son to help her now.

She picked the tea up and inhaled the delicate scent. She often drank camomile tea on an evening. She stood by the window and gazed out as she drank the tea. She could see the roofs of neighbouring houses. They didn't seem that far away. A mile or two? She could call on them later, and ask if she could phone DCI Dexter. Was he trustworthy? She didn't know, but he was all she had. She didn't want to phone Sam at the hospital, not if he was recovering. It wasn't fair to get him further involved.

But she was still half hoping he'd track her down.

She finished the tea and then got into the pyjamas and dressing gown. They were big on her, but they were clean. Her damp hair hung on her shoulders, so Maggie started looking for a hairdryer. She didn't find one anywhere in the guest room, so she left it and headed into the room next to it. This one was much larger and had fewer crystals decorating it.

Out of habit, Maggie opened the wardrobe door because that's where she kept her hairdryer at home. She quickly scanned the colourful clothes hanging there. She winced slightly at all the silver dresses. Sonia certainly was keen on that colour.

Maggie froze.

What was that?

She touched the item which had caught her attention.

That looked like... No, it couldn't be.

But look at that tartan coat next to it.

And those trousers.

This couldn't be a coincidence.

Maggie's hand shook as she closed the wardrobe door.

Just how well did Carmella know her friend Sonia?

Chapter 53

The killer looked upwards. She smiled as she heard Maggie moving about in the room above. Nosy thing. She'll be putting all the pieces together soon. It had taken her long enough.

The killer turned her attention to Oscar who was sitting in the chair opposite her. She said, "We need to be gentle with your mum, after all she's been through. She was almost shot in Whitby, you know. But that annoying friend of hers got in the way. He must have seen the red dot of my gun on your mum's chest. It was in Whitby where your mum nearly ended her life. It would have made the local news." She sighed heavily. "But she survived. Shame."

Oscar's head lolled to one side. His eyes fluttered before closing. He wasn't listening. The killer tutted. How rude.

The door behind her opened. The killer turned around and gave Maggie a beaming smile.

Those pyjamas she was wearing looked hideous. And that dressing gown made Maggie's wan face look even paler.

Maggie stuttered, "I...I never told you about the shooting in Whitby. How do you know about that?"

"Come closer," the killer beckoned her in. "We've got a lot to talk about."

Maggie's legs gave way, and she slithered to the carpet. She gave the killer a confused look. "Carmella? What's going on? And what did you put in my tea?"

Carmella walked over to Maggie and knelt at her side. She pushed a lock of hair away from Maggie's face. "Just a little something to make you docile. Dear Maggie, you poor love. You should have gone to Brighton when I suggested it. But you didn't. And now you're involved with something that isn't going to end well for you."

Maggie struggled to speak. "Carmella..." She passed out.

Chapter 54

Maggie felt nauseous as she came to her senses later. She was sitting on a wooden chair, and it took her a minute to work out where she was. She soon wished she hadn't.

She was in a damp-smelling cellar. A single light bulb dangling from the ceiling did a dismal job of illuminating the room, and Maggie couldn't see into the corners of the room.

Maggie took in all in. Paint peeling from the crumbling walls. Large watermarks dotted across the ceiling. Cobwebs hanging like delicate decoration from various broken pieces of furniture. The floor covered in dirt, with little paw prints crisscrossing it.

As Maggie tried to make sense of where she was, another realisation made her stomach tighten in fear. She was tied to the wooden chair she was sitting on. Her hands were positioned behind the back of the chair, and her ankles were fastened to the front legs.

The person who had tied her to the chair stepped out of a dark corner. Maggie almost didn't recognise her. Gone were the blue hair and hazel eyes. The long, colourful dress had gone too. Carmella's hair was now short and white, her eyes were dark brown, and she was wearing tight blue jeans and a black T-shirt with an image of a dagger on it.

Carmella gave Maggie a nasty smirk as she sauntered closer. "It's about time you came round. You've been out for ages. I had to drag your hefty body down the cellar steps. I thought you were on a diet? If you are, it's not working. Not that it matters now." She pulled a chair up, and sat opposite Maggie. She gave her a long look as if studying her.

Maggie attempted to wriggle her hands free behind her. But the ropes only cut tighter into her wrists. She looked at Carmella. She could only think of one question. "Why?"

"Why what?"

"Why have you tied me up?"

"To stop you running away, of course."

"Where's Oscar? What have you done to him?" Anger rose in Maggie. "You'd better not have hurt him!"

Carmella shrugged. "I haven't hurt him. Not yet. You'll see him soon. I really, really wished you'd gone to Brighton, Maggie. If you had, you wouldn't have seen me putting an end to Phelps. I didn't want you on the street when I murdered him in case you were staring out of the window like you do all the time. Nosy thing. Why didn't you go to Brighton, Maggie? Was it because you were too scared to leave the safety of your house and the street? Hmm? You're like a scared little rabbit down its rabbit hole. So timid. So fearful of change."

Maggie stiffened. She wasn't feeling timid now. "I want to see my son right now!"

"No. You'll see him when I'm ready. Don't you want to know why I killed William Phelps the other night?"

"No. I want to see Oscar."

Carmella tutted. "Stop going on about your pathetic son. I'll tell you why I killed William Phelps. Of course, you know that isn't his real name. Those friends of yours did a good job of finding out about him. Too good a job. I'm glad they're both in hospital. I'm almost tempted to pay them a visit and mess with their medication. Oh! Maggie, I nearly forgot. That tracking device in your handbag? The one that Sam put there? He's very handsome, by the way. Quite charming. It's a terrible shame you won't see each other again. Anyway, I've jammed the device. It was when I gave you a hug outside Phelps' house earlier. I slipped something in your bag to jam the signal." She held her hands out. "So, if you're expecting Sam to come to your rescue, you're going to be disappointed."

Maggie did feel disappointed, but she tried not to show it.

Carmella carried on. "Phelps used to work for me. I thought he was loyal, but he betrayed me. A couple of others betrayed me too. I got rid of them months ago. The police protection programme didn't help them, and it didn't help Phelps either. Do you know how they betrayed me, Maggie?"

Maggie didn't answer. She was trying to look for an escape route. She could only see one exit door at the top of a set of wooden stairs behind Carmella.

"They did a jewellers' job," Carmella said. "Without my knowledge, or approval. Thought they could do jobs on the side without me finding out. Of course, being the idiots they are," she grimaced, "sorry, the idiots they were, the police caught them. And then the cowards turned against me. Said they would give away my identity, and that of people I work with. I couldn't have that.

You understand, don't you? It's taken me decades to set up my many streams of income. I was not going to give that up because of those fools."

Maggie tried to look as if she were listening. The door at the top of the stairs was ajar. Did it lead to the kitchen? She hadn't noticed a door in the kitchen earlier, but she'd been too busy looking for a phone. Were they even in the same house?

Carmella suddenly slapped her leg. "Maggie, you should have seen Phelps' face when he saw me on our street. He thought he'd moved to a safe area, but he hadn't! I made sure he was moved into that house. If you haven't worked it out by now, I've got a few contacts in the police force. That's how I found out about your hedgehog camera. I bet you were wondering about that, weren't you?"

"Who are your contacts?" Maggie asked as pleasantly as she could. How was she supposed to get out of her bondage? She couldn't make a run for it if she was tied to the chair. A trickle of fear went down her spine. She had a feeling she wouldn't get the chance to escape.

Carmella wagged a finger at Maggie. "I'm not going to tell you who my contacts are. But I can tell you it's not that lovely DCI Dexter, or his girlfriend, Ingrid. Fancy her being Sam's ex-wife! That's a bit of a pickle, isn't it? If we were still friends, we could discuss that over a bottle of wine or two. I'm going to miss our cosy chats."

"I won't. Were we ever friends?"

Carmella made a rocking motion with her hand. "Sort of. I don't really have friends. I did enjoy our time together. Apart from all the whining you did. And all the boring talks we had! Maggie, you talk about the same things over and over again. You never do anything new. You've been living the same life every day for years."

Maggie gave her a cold look but didn't say anything.

"Let's talk about me now. I was telling you about Phelps. Yes, his face when he saw me on the street. He was petrified! He knew there was no escape. I planted some items in his house just to let him know I was watching him. A bit like I did with you and those T-shirts. Those cost me a fortune, by the way. The funniest thing I did to Phelps was taking a photo of him while he was asleep! Using his own phone! That must have given him such a fright when he saw that photo. His nerves were in tatters when I finally put an end to him. He did attempt to tell the police, of course, but he didn't get far with that thanks to my contacts."

"You tried to kill me in Whitby. Why?"

"Why are you asking such stupid questions? You're not a stupid person."

"I want to know."

"Because you were getting too close to the truth. As much as I was enjoying our game of cat and mouse, it was taking up my valuable time." She frowned. "I'm so annoyed with Sam getting in the way in Whitby. But I did enjoy hearing you scream like that. You were hysterical. It made me laugh."

"Have you finished gloating yet? Can I see Oscar now?"

"Not yet. We haven't talked about those disguises you found in the wardrobe upstairs. I knew you'd go nosing around. You can't help yourself."

Maggie recalled the items she'd seen. The tartan coat. The battered backpack. Other items of clothing she'd noticed people on her many train journeys wearing. She said, "You've been following me everywhere."

Carmella gave her a gleeful smile. "I have. I had never been to Morecambe before. I enjoyed the fish and chips there. Yum. Have you worked out my so-called friend Sonia doesn't exist? I'm sure you have. Thanks to my many streams of income, I've got various properties around the country, including this house and the one in Brighton. Oh! Maggie, did you like my acting earlier? In my garden? When I pretended I'd been shot? I thought I was amazing. I had to nick my ear to get it to bleed, but it was worth it."

"Where did the gunshot come from?" As soon as she'd asked the question, Maggie regretted it. Was Carmella concealing a gun somewhere on her person? Was she going to produce it with a flourish at any moment?

Carmella replied, "I made the noise from an app on my phone. Modern technology is amazing. You haven't asked what line of business I'm in. Aren't you interested?"

"No."

"I'll tell you anyway. It's not very exciting, but it pays the bills. It's drugs. I sell them at the fairs I go to. I hide them inside the many things I sell. It's so easy to sell them. And you've helped me, Maggie. Do you remember all the times you've taken packages in for me? So kind of you. They were mainly drugs. Not the Amazon boxes. Those were genuine. The other boxes were full of drugs. Thanks so much for taking them in."

Maggie felt sick. She'd taken in hundreds of boxes for Carmella over the fourteen years they'd known each other.

Carmella tapped her chin. "Have we covered everything? I think we have. Have you got any questions? Anything I've missed out?"

"Where's Oscar?"

"Stop asking me that!" Carmella snapped. Then she leaned back in her chair and laced her hands behind her head. A slow, devious smile came to her face. "I'm sorry about your husband, Maggie."

Maggie frowned. "What do you mean?"

"Your handsome husband. I'm sorry about him." She paused. Her smile grew. "I'm sorry I killed him that night. I'd had too much to drink. I shouldn't have been driving. But you know what it's like at Christmas. You get lost in the festivities and think one more drink won't hurt. But it did hurt. It hurt your husband. Sorry. I crashed right into poor Harry. He never stood a chance."

"It was you? The driver of the other car was you?" Maggie could hardly get her words out.

Carmella continued smiling. "Oopsie."

Chapter 55

Maggie couldn't take in the horror of everything. Carmella's deceit and betrayal. The heartless way she'd admitting to killing her husband. And the fear of not knowing where her son was. She struggled again with the ties on her hands, but to no avail.

Carmella stood up. "I only moved to your street so I could watch you grieve. And to see if you'd be any use to me. You were an easy target. You needed someone to listen to your woes, and to wipe your sad tears away. It didn't take you long to trust me, and to then take packages in for me. I almost started to care for you. But, to be honest, you got on my nerves. You moaned about your sad life, but you never did anything about it. You never had the courage to have an adventure. But you're having one now! Thanks to me." She bowed her head. "You are very welcome."

"Stop talking. Just stop talking," Maggie mumbled.

"I will do soon. And so will you. Let me get your soppy son for you. Oscar! Are you still there?" She walked towards one of the dark corners. There was a shuffling sound, and then Carmella came out of the darkness pushing Oscar on a wheeled chair. His hands were tied and resting on his lap.

Maggie's heart missed a beat. "Oscar! Why isn't he moving? Why are his eyes closed?"

Carmella patted Oscar's head. "He's dying. Poor love. He hasn't got long left." Her face brightened. "But at least you get to spend your last moments with him. Not like you did with your husband. There was only me watching Harry's life drain away that night. I suppose I could have phoned for help. I might have saved him. But we'll never know now."

Maggie blinked away her tears. "What have you done to Oscar?"

"Poisoned him. Just enough so he'll die slowly. I wanted you to watch him die. I wish I could stay and watch, but I've got things to do. Busy, busy! First of all, I've got to deal with that bad-tempered woman on our street. After all I've done for her over the years too. I've provided her with free accommodation when I needed a house to look occupied, and this is how she repays me. I can't have her telling the police about your conversation, and me turning up like that. And I need to collect my things from my house on Lilac Lane. I can't stay there

160

now." She put her hands on her hips. "I really wish you'd gone to Brighton. You've messed everything up. I might have to leave the country. Maggie, you nuisance."

"Don't do this, Carmella. You don't have to kill Oscar. Please. Don't do this." Maggie's tears ran freely down her cheeks.

"I do have to do this, Maggie, my old friend. But you won't be sad for too long. Oh! I nearly forgot. I don't know where my head is today. Hang on a mo." She dashed away to a dark corner, and came back with a large timer. She pressed some buttons, and then placed the timer on the floor next to Oscar's chair.

Maggie noticed the time. "Why is it counting down?" She swallowed. "Is that how long Oscar's got left?"

Carmella gave her a cheerful nod. "Yes. And you too. In ten minutes, I'm going to blow up this charming house. I have to. It's got your DNA all over it." She gave Maggie an annoyed look. "I'm not happy about doing this, Maggie. Destroying my house, I mean, not killing you two. You've served your purpose. It's time to move on. Can you see the timer okay? What about your darling son? Shall I push him a bit closer? Would you like to kiss him goodbye?" She manoeuvred Oscar until he was right next to Maggie. "If you slap his face, he might come round a bit. Slap him hard. Oh! Silly me. I forgot that you can't move your hands. My head's all over the place today."

Maggie tried once more. "Please, please don't do this."

"I have to. I think I might actually miss you." She grinned. "But I'll get over it. Goodbye, Maggie Kelburn. It's been fun." She blew Maggie a kiss and then ran up the steps. She closed the door behind her, and Maggie heard a lock sliding into place.

Maggie stared helplessly at the timer. Less than nine minutes left of her life.

Chapter 56

Maggie wasn't going without a fight. Whilst Carmella had been gloating, she'd been trying to think of an escape plan. She remembered those stories Sam had told her in Morecambe about his early days working in the surveillance industry, and the predicaments he'd found himself in. He'd been tied to chairs more than once but had managed to wiggle his way free by stretching the rope over and over again until it had given way a little. Maggie didn't have time for that. Or the muscles. On some occasions, he'd produced a small knife which he kept on his person at all times. But Maggie didn't have one of those useful knives on her person.

Eight minutes.

How was she supposed to get out of this?

She wiggled back and forth on the chair. It creaked a little. She quickly examined it. The chair was old. Could she break it? How? Throw herself around the floor frantically? She might cause more damage to herself than the chair if she did that.

The walls! Hadn't she seen a film where someone had thrown themselves at a wall and broken a chair they'd been tied to? Had it worked?

Seven minutes.

Maggie looked at Oscar before clumsily lifting herself half off the chair. Her arms screamed in protest at the unnatural position they were now in. Maggie ignored the pain shooting up her arms, and shuffled over to the wall. She turned around and attempted to whack the chair against the wall. She had no idea what she was doing, but it was better than doing nothing.

Whack! Whack!

Looking at the still figure of her son gave Maggie strength she didn't know she had. Over and over, she bashed the chair into the wall at various angles She caught her tied hands a few times against the wall, and fresh pain went through her.

Whack! Whack! Crack!

Something cracked.

The front leg broke away from the chair. Her ankle was still tied to it, but she could now move her leg more freely.

Now what?

Five minutes.

After a couple of collisions with the wall, the back legs of the chair eventually broke and fell off. A few more whacks, and the back of the chair came away altogether. Maggie's aching arms now rested against her back. How was she supposed to untie them?

She bashed the remaining parts of the chair until her other leg was free.

Three minutes.

In despair, Maggie took in her situation. Half-broken chair legs were tied to her ankles, and her hands were bound tightly behind her back. She needed to get them in front of her somehow. Then she could have a go at dragging Oscar up the steps. And by some miracle, she would have to get the locked door open.

Maggie sat down and rolled to her side. Perhaps she could pull her hands over her bottom and then up in front of her? But she wasn't double-jointed. And she wasn't a yoga expert who could put their body into impossible poses.

But she did have two pieces of sharp wood attached firmly to her ankles. Could she rub the rope against them until the wood cut through the rope?

It was worth a try.

Maggie got herself into an uncomfortable position so that her hands were near the wood on her left leg. Then she got to work, hoping against hope that something would happen.

Very soon, something did happen.

Chapter 57

With the continuous rubbing of rope against the wood, Maggie's binds began to feel looser. Had she cut through enough rope? She twisted her hands frantically until the rope fell off.

One minute left on the timer.

She didn't have time to untie her feet. She stood up and shuffled over to Oscar. The sharp parts of the chair legs dug into her skin.

"Oscar! Can you hear me? Oscar!" She slapped his face and pulled on his arms. There was no response. She didn't have time to untie him. She slapped him again. "Oscar! Please! It's Mum. Open your eyes. I need your help. Oscar!"

His eyes fluttered, and then he opened them. He gave her a lazy smile. "Mum. Hi. I love you."

Maggie attempted to pull him off the chair. It was like trying to move a huge sack of cement. "Oscar! Get up! We have to get out of here. Help me. I can't lift you."

"Mum, I don't feel well."

"I know you don't. Can you stand up?"

"I'll try."

With Maggie's help, he got unsteadily to his feet. He asked, "Am I drunk? Mum, where are we? Am I dreaming?"

"No, love. This isn't a dream. Can you walk up those steps?" Maggie sagged under the weight of him.

He blinked. "I don't think I can. Let me sit down. I'm tired. I want to sleep."

Maggie moved him over to the steps. "Try to get up the steps. Please, love. Try."

"Okay."

A deafening buzz came from the timer as it reached zero.

Time was up.

Maggie braced herself for the explosion. She looked at Oscar, and said, "I love you."

Chapter 58

Nothing happened. No explosion. No big bang.

But Maggie knew Carmella wanted them dead. Maybe the timer was out a little, and the explosion would come soon.

With as much strength as she could manage, Maggie pulled Oscar up the steps. Oscar kept moaning and saying he wanted to sleep.

"Just one more step," Maggie coaxed him. She was dripping with sweat, and the sharp splints were repeatedly digging into her legs.

They managed to reach the last step. All they had to do now was bash this door down. That's all.

Maggie leaned Oscar against the door while she got her breath back. She would have to throw herself at the door over and over again until she broke it down. That happened all the time in the movies, didn't it?

She could do it. She'd keep going until the door was open. Or the house had exploded.

Oscar sleepily put his tied hands on the handle. "Mum, where are we? Where does this door go?" He wiggled the handle. To Maggie's surprise, the door opened. It hadn't been locked at all. But Maggie had heard the noise of it locking. Hadn't she? Or had Carmella used another app to fool her?

That didn't matter now.

Oscar wavered on his feet and looked like he was going to faint. Maggie grabbed him, kicked the door fully open, and pulled him through.

She half expected Carmella to be standing there with a gun in her hand, and a satisfied smile on her face.

But Carmella wasn't there. And her car wasn't outside either.

Maggie grunted with effort as she dragged Oscar out of the house and towards the lane.

That was when the house exploded.

Chapter 59

Maggie stared helplessly at her son. She loved him so much. She couldn't imagine life without him. Tears ran down her cheeks. She didn't know she could cry so much.

A warm hand rested gently on her shoulder. Sam said, "He's going to be okay. You know that, don't you?"

Maggie kept her eyes on Oscar as she nodded in response. "But he nearly died. I nearly lost him. I can't stop thinking about that."

"But he didn't die. He's in the best place. The nurses are taking good care of him. And the doctor has explained about his injuries, and how he's on the mend."

Maggie wiped tears away from one eye. "They said he was lucky to be alive." She looked at Sam. "He got the brunt of the explosion. It should have been me. I should have protected him. That's my job. I'm his mum."

Sam squeezed her shoulder gently. "Maggie, you dragged him out of the cellar. Any longer, and you would have both been in the house when it blew up. You saved him. And you injured yourself in the process."

Maggie shrugged. "My injuries don't matter. I should never have trusted Carmella. I should have known there was something evil about her. I should have kept her well away from my son. I should have—" Her voice broke, and she turned her attention back to Oscar. There were too many tubes going into him. Too many cuts and bruises on him.

But Sam was right. Oscar was going to be okay.

"Maggie, let me get you a coffee. When did you last have something to eat?"

She gave him a tired smile. "I can't remember. I can't leave Oscar's side. He needs me."

"He's asleep. You won't be much use to him when he wakes up if you're about to faint from hunger. Come on; we'll be ten minutes. And I'll let the nurses know where we are in case he wakes up."

"I don't know."

Sam put his arm around her shoulder. "Let me take care of you for ten minutes. Just ten minutes."

Maggie relented. "Okay."

As they walked away from Oscar's bed, Maggie couldn't help but look left and right, and then over her shoulder.

Sam said, "You don't have to do that. Carmella is behind bars. And she won't be getting out for years. You're safe."

"I don't think I'll ever feel safe again. Are you sure she's behind bars? I know DCI Dexter told me that, but have you checked?"

"I did." His expression hardened. "I'm still furious with Tyler Dexter. He should have chased up some of his leads against Carmella earlier. It wasn't just drugs she was selling, like she told you. She was behind many murders and cyber crimes which have been going on for years around the UK. Many people worked for her. Tyler should have made the connection earlier. He should have taken that footage of yours seriously. Then she wouldn't have imprisoned you. And you wouldn't have nearly died."

Maggie looked into his concerned face. "Hey, don't you start worrying about things that didn't happen. That's my speciality." He still had his arm around her shoulders, but she didn't mind.

"Sorry. But I'm annoyed. He could have arrested her days ago if he'd done his job properly. None of this needed to happen."

"But it did." Her eyes suddenly stung. "I always wanted to know who killed Harry, and now I do. I keep going over Carmella's gloating words. How could she be so cold-hearted?"

Sam shook his head. "I wish I could give you an answer, but I can't. Some people are just evil."

They carried on walking. Maggie didn't know whether to say what was on her mind or not. But she wasn't as timid as she used to be. She said, "Sam, I know this has been a horrible time. And we've both nearly died. And our sons have been injured. Is Jake still okay, by the way?"

"Yes. He was fine yesterday when you asked me, and he's still fine. He's back at work. Go on. What were you saying?"

They stopped walking. Sam took his arm back, and they turned to look at each other.

Maggie said, "I'm glad I met you. I can't thank you enough for helping me. And for saving my life in Whitby."

"You saved my life too when I followed you and Jake. And you took care of my van as well. I love that van." He smiled. "I'm glad I met you too. We've had quite the adventure, haven't we?"

"We have." She lowered her voice. "Have you found out who Carmella's police contacts are yet?"

Sam shook his head. "But it's a matter of time." He suddenly looked nervous. "When Oscar has fully recovered, and he's out of hospital, do you think we—"

He was interrupted by a nurse. "Ms Kelburn, your son is awake. He wants to see you."

"I'd better go. Do you want to come with me? You haven't officially met Oscar yet."

"I can't, sorry. I have to get back to the shop. We're inundated with work. Maggie, can we meet again soon?"

Maggie gave him a direct look. She smiled for the first time in days. It was time for her to have more adventures, to take more chances. "We will meet again, Sam. We'll meet again very soon. I'll make sure of that."

THE END

The next story in the Maggie Kelburn series is A Murder Hunt. Read on for chapters 1 and 2

A Murder Hunt
Chapter 1

Maggie looked out of her kitchen window. She was watching the trees in the public lane beyond her back garden.

Something wasn't right out there.

The branches of one tree were swaying. But the ones either side of it weren't moving.

Maggie's eyes narrowed. Now look. That tree was now moving rapidly as if caught in a strong wind. What was wrong with it? Was it about to fall over? She hoped not. It was a tall tree, and if it fell it would land on her garden fence.

She tutted. She'd been on to the council many times about those trees, and how big they had grown. But had they done anything about it? No, they hadn't. And now the trees had grown out of control.

The branches of the left-hand side of the moving tree shifted. A face peered out.

Maggie stiffened.

Someone was in the tree.

The person looked Maggie's way, and then ducked back into the foliage.

Instead of feeling scared, Maggie was furious. Someone was spying on her. Again. And she wasn't going to put up with it.

Maggie stormed towards the kitchen door. Hadn't she been through enough last month? All that business with her neighbour being murdered. And then her having to go on the run from the killer.

She wasn't going through all that again. No, thank you.

She paused at the kitchen door, turned around and grabbed the nearest weapon she could find. Then she headed out of the door and into the back garden.

The tree was still moving, but not so much now. Maggie could see the man halfway up it more clearly. He was wearing dark clothes, but she could see his thin, bearded face. And he had his hair pulled up in one of those man-bun things.

Maggie marched along the garden path, and brandished her rolling pin at the tree. "Hey! You! In the tree. I can see you."

The startled man looked her way. He was only a young man, probably in his early twenties. He attempted to shuffle back into the branches.

Maggie stood at the end of her garden. "Don't try to hide. What are you doing? Are you spying on me? Get down from that tree right now and explain yourself."

She looked up and down the public lane. There was no one else around. It was a Tuesday, and Maggie knew her immediate neighbours were out and wouldn't be home until early evening.

She lowered the rolling pin as she realised the danger she'd put herself in. She backed up, and called out less confidently, "I'm going to phone the police. Stay right where you are."

There was a loud rustling, followed by the cracking noise of small branches breaking.

Maggie yelped as the man suddenly dropped to the ground a few feet away. He landed expertly on his feet. He turned to Maggie, winked at her, and then raced off down the lane.

Maggie was too stunned to speak for a moment. Blooming cheek! Spying on her like that. Some people didn't have any manners. She would report him to the police. And she'd give them a full description. She was good at remembering faces, and she'd got a good look at that cheeky man's face.

She was about to walk away when something caught her eye. What was that at the bottom of the tree? Something was glittering in the grass.

Maggie checked the lane again, tightened her grip on the rolling pin, and stepped out of the garden.

She moved over to the tree and knelt at the side of it. What were those?

Maggie picked up one of the items. It was a gold-coloured plastic coin. It had a smiley face on it.

Had the cheeky man dropped it?

There were two other coins on the grass which looked identical. Maggie picked those up too. A quick search of the ground didn't reveal any other coins.

Maggie straightened up and glanced upwards and through the branches of the tree. She noticed a few twisted branches. That must have been where the man was hiding. Had he been spying on her? Or had he been up there for another reason?

She should phone the police. Yes, that would be the sensible thing to do. Or she could...

Maggie smiled as another thought came to her. That sounded like a better idea.

And it would give her the perfect excuse to see him again.

Chapter 2

The butterflies in Maggie's stomach were having a merry old dance as she entered Ward's Surveillance Supplies an hour later. She didn't know why she felt so nervous. Sam Ward was just a man; just a friend. That was all. Nothing more.

Her butterflies disagreed and fluttered some more when she saw Sam. He was sitting at a computer behind a desk at the other side of the shop. That dark blue suit he was wearing accentuated his slim, athletic build. His light brown eyes looked her way, and he broke into a wide smile causing crinkles to appear around his brown eyes in the most charming way.

Maggie swallowed nervously and gave him a shy smile. She didn't know why she felt this nervous when she was with Sam. He was just a friend.

"Maggie. Hi!" Sam stood up and walked towards her, still smiling. He stopped in front of her. "How are you? How's Oscar doing? Is he still at home recovering?"

"He went back to Newcastle yesterday. I don't think he had recovered nearly enough, and I told him that. But he told me to stop fussing. And I told him it was my job as his mother. Then he said—" She abruptly stopped, and let out a nervous laugh. "Sorry. You didn't need to know all that. Oscar is fine, thank you. How are you?"

"Fine. Thank you. And you?"

"Fine. Thank you."

They smiled at each other.

Maggie broke the silence. "I'm here for professional advice."

A look of disappointment came into Sam's eyes. "Oh? This isn't a personal visit?"

"Well, yes and no. I wanted to say thank you for coming to see Oscar while he was recovering. And for all those magazines you brought him. It was kind of you."

Sam shrugged. "It was nothing. He'd been through a tough time. So had you. I wanted to make sure you were both fine. That's all."

Maggie nodded. "We appreciated it." She paused. She had meant to invite Sam out for a meal to say thank you for his kindness. Not a date, just a meal. But she hadn't found the courage to ask him yet.

"Is there something you wanted to ask me?" Sam prompted her.

Maggie shook her head. The courage to ask him out for a meal still hadn't appeared.

"But you said you were here on a business matter," Sam said. "Would you like to take a seat and tell me what's on your mind? Can I get you a hot drink? Or water?"

"A tea would be nice, thank you." Maggie followed Sam over to the desk. He pulled out a chair for her, and she sat down. She glanced around the shop at the surveillance equipment displayed on glass shelves. It was far too clinical-looking in this shop, and too open. If someone wanted to discuss a problem of an intimate nature, they would have to do it in front of any other customers. Not that there were any other customers in here at the moment. In fact, Maggie had never seen customers in here. How did Sam get business?

She jumped as something was placed in front of her.

"Here's your tea," Sam said with a smile.

"Thanks. I didn't even you notice you leaving the room to get it."

He grinned. "I'm a tea-making ninja. I'm empty-handed one minute, and in the blink of an eye, I'm handing you a cuppa." He moved to the opposite side of the desk and sat down. "What can I help you with?"

Maggie pulled the gold-coloured plastic coins from her bag and placed them on the table. "I found these."

He frowned as he picked one up. "Where? Inside a Christmas cracker? It's a bit early for Christmas shopping, isn't it?"

It was July, and not too early in Maggie's opinion. But she didn't tell Sam that.

She continued, "I found them at the bottom of a tree."

"Okay." He nodded as if that were normal.

"The tree is in that public lane at the bottom of my garden."

He nodded again. "I have noticed those trees. They need pruning."

"I know. I've phoned the council many times."

Sam said, "Phone them again. Tell them about this littering business as well."

"Littering?"

He held the plastic coin up. "This?"

"Oh no, that's not littering. At least, I don't think so. I suspect it was the man in the tree who dropped them."

Sam blinked and lowered the coin. "What man?"

"The man in the tree. I thought he was spying on me. But I'm not so sure now." She took a sip of tea. "You make a lovely cup of tea."

Sam leaned forward on the desk. "Maggie, are you telling me there was a strange man in a tree, at the end of your garden, and he might have been spying on you?"

She nodded. "He might have something to do with these coins. I found them when he jumped out of the tree and ran away. I think I scared him with my rolling pin." She took another drink of tea.

"Rolling pin?"

"Yes, I threatened him with it. Well, sort of. I waved it at him. I wouldn't actually hit someone with it." She considered the matter. "Unless it was in self-defence."

A muscle twitched in Sam's jaw. In a voice devoid of emotion, he said, "Am I right in assuming you approached a strange man in a tree?"

Maggie nodded.

"Were you on your own?"

She nodded again. She didn't like the look in Sam's eyes.

"On your own with only a rolling pin to protect you?"

Maggie's nod was less certain. "Erm, yes. But when I realised I might be in danger, I told him I was going to phone the police."

"I'm glad to hear that," Sam said tightly.

"That's when he jumped out of the tree, winked at me, and then ran off."

"He winked at you?" Sam's hand tightened around the coin.

"Be careful," Maggie pointed at the coin. "Don't break it."

Sam put the coin down. He let out a long sigh. "Maggie, that was a dangerous situation you put yourself in. You could have been hurt."

"I know, but I wasn't hurt."

"But you could have been. You need to take care of yourself."

Maggie was touched by his concern, but her defensive side came out. She sat up straighter. "I can take care of myself. I didn't come here for a lecture on personal safety. Do you recognise those plastic coins?"

Sam held her gaze for a moment before giving his attention back to the coins. "I've never seen them before."

"I have," said a cheery voice behind Maggie.

Maggie almost jumped out of her skin. She looked at the young man behind her. "Jake! You scared the life out of me. I never heard you come in."

He grinned, looking just like his dad. "I'm like a ninja. Light on my feet." He threw a wrapped packaged towards Sam. "Dad, they didn't have any bacon sandwiches left, so I got you a sausage one."

"Thanks. I'll save it for later." Sam pointed to the coins. "You've seen these before, then?"

Jake pushed his floppy blonde hair off his face, and perched on the end of the desk. "Who found them?"

"I did," Maggie admitted.

Jake took a sharp intake of breath. "Big mistake. I would not like to be in your shoes right now."

A note from the author

I hope you enjoyed this story. If you did, would you be able to post a quick review, please? Thank you, I really appreciate it.

This story has been checked for errors. If you do spot any errors I would love it if you could email me to let me know about them – thank you.

Sign up to my newsletter and you will receive 4 short mystery stories as a thank you. You can sign up here: www.gillianlarkin.co.uk[1]

You can email me at: gillian@gillianlarkin.com

Best wishes
Gillian

---

1.   http://www.gillianlarkin.co.uk

I Know What You Saw
A Maggie Kelburn Mystery
(Book 1)
By
GILLIAN LARKIN
www.gillianlarkin.co.uk[2]

2. http://www.gillianlarkin.co.uk